Three Wooden Crosses

DAVID C. HALL

WESTBOW*
PRESS
A DIVISION OF THOMAS NELSON
& ZONDERVAN

WestBow Press books may be ordered through booksellers or by contacting:

WestBow Press
A Division of Thomas Nelson & Zondervan
1663 Liberty Drive
Bloomington, IN 47403
www.westbowpress.com
1 (866) 928-1240

ISBN: 978-1-4908-6204-0 (sc)
ISBN: 978-1-4908-6205-7 (hc)
ISBN: 978-1-4908-6222-4 (e)

Library of Congress Control Number: 2014921435

Printed in the United States of America.

WestBow Press rev. date: 12/1/2014

To my wife, Alicia, and to my three little
girls, Rylyn, Zaley, and Marlowe.

God shows me His wondrous love every day by
allowing me the privilege of loving you.

Acknowledgment

I would like to thank Randy Travis, Kim Williams, and Doug Johnson for their Christian song, "Three Wooden Crosses." The song inspired the characters of this story and provided me a context to share a story put in my heart by our loving God.

Thanks to my loving wife, Alicia, who has served as consoler, cheerleader, reality checker, pastor, counselor, editor, and friend. Without you, this book would not have been possible.

Early on, my brother-in-law gave me the push I needed to venture into the crowdsourcing realm. Without his help in getting the campaign together, I am not sure it ever would have gotten off the ground. Thank you, P. J.

Finally, thanks to all of those who supported this project from the beginning on Kickstarter. You had faith enough in the project to give your money blindly. I cannot tell you how much your encouragement meant to me. Thank you:

Jen and Mike Akers
Caroline and Dan Bartlett
Philip R. and Marge Butler
P. J.

Bryan and Missy Brading
Kathryn Brown
Carlos and Vicki Canales
Mickey and Lovenia Casto

Dayton and Barbara Carpenter
Susan Cornell
The Cramer family
Leron Culbreath
Chris Davis
Dean and Holly DeFord
Ryan and Jillian Eaton
Ann Eischeid
Dana
Tracy Todd Etu
Michelle Fletcher
Guadalupe J. Flores
Brent Goers
Luke, Stephanie, Alexandra,
	and Jackson
I. V. and Susan Hall
Tom and Jeanne Hall (Mom
	and Dad)
Bill and Sharon Hall
Mark and Connie Hall

Chris Haynes
Jack and Melana Hydrick
Kristi Jones
Matt and Melissa Kramer
Jim and Angie Lichty
Michelle Rider Miller
Aunt Kay
The Paul family
Debby and Herb Peters
Arturo Jay Pua
Jason, Suzy, and Piper
David and Cherry Ross
Danny and Mary Beth Scango
Shawn Scango
David Schuyler
Lisa Scott and family
Kathryn Seybert
John Smith
Becky and John Smith
Florine Witherspoon

Prologue

2012

Pastor Jones turned slowly and shielded his eyes from the bright midsummer sun. The light was beautiful coming from behind the small brick church as it illuminated the steeple, making it seem much taller than it actually was. The rays of sun bounced playfully off the small, stained-glass windows, which made their way around the church. On each window, a scene depicting the life and ministry of Jesus was pictured. Pastor Jones looked at each scene discerningly as he recalled the Scripture associated with the colorful art.

A small breeze came from the west and blew gently against the pastor's back. He closed his eyes and engaged all of his other senses to better experience the breath of the Lord. As the smile on his face was widening, Tom Jenkins approached from behind him and put his hand on the pastor's shoulder.

"Good morning, Preacher. Sure is going to be a wonderful day," he said.

"Yes, Tom," Pastor Jones replied. "Today is certainly a special day."

In the church, the congregation gathered with whispers of anticipation. Pastor Jones had indicated that today was a miraculous occasion. "An occasion of God's demonstrated masterpiece," he had said to all in the church last Sunday. Yet no one in the church could think of what event would lead Pastor Jones to make such a fuss.

The church had been erected in 1975, but the building was dedicated in the winter, making it the wrong season for an anniversary of that event. Nonetheless, Levi Forester made sure to let everyone know he remembered every word of the dedication ceremony because he had been the first to ring the bell encased in the steeple. No one commented to Levi that the bell hadn't worked in years. It still looked beautiful, especially in the sunlight, but it had not called the beginning of a service in ten years, at least.

Mary Parker, the church secretary, thought that she had the answer as she searched for Pastor Jones's baptismal record. The church always kept those records on file and, being a pastor, it would be a date special to him. Earlier in the week, she had searched through his records and pulled a copy of the certificate.

It looked like he had been baptized at a small church in Texas, in a town she had never heard of. The attached picture showed Pastor Jones as a young boy and the date was February 22, but no year was provided. Ms. Mary wrinkled her lips and placed the document back in the folder with a sigh.

The church had brewed with excitement throughout the week. The anticipation of the anniversary event was partnered with the anxiousness and wonderment of guessing the surprise, and it all began to energize the congregation. Twenty-nine of the thirty people in the choir had shown up for practice on Wednesday. It was a far cry from the ten to twelve singers who regularly filled the music room.

Cliff Lazenby, the worship leader, was positive that the sudden interest had more to do with having a front-row seat on Sunday than with leading people to Calvary with song. But nonetheless, he was glad to have them there as he took in the wonderful and powerful sound of a full choir.

The youth group, not to be outdone by the choir, made signs for the event and hung them around the church in celebration. The vagueness of the signs was proof that no one had a clue what the church was celebrating; however, they revealed the expectation of a magnificent purpose for sure.

The sign inside the entrance to the church read, "God Is Wonderful and His Works Are Mighty." The sign outside the choir room read, "Sing Alleluia for God's Wondrous Works." Outside the sanctuary doors, a third sign instructed worshippers to "Enter to Hear the Miraculous Stories of a Compassionate God." Though they were truly ambiguous, the signs certainly got the point across. Pastor Jones chuckled as he read the last sign and entered the sanctuary.

Chapter 1

1962

The anguished eyes stared vacantly at him through the black mix of sand, salt water, and blood that had formed a mask over the soldier's face. He reached to grab his canteen so he could provide the young man one last drink, but as he turned, the soldier grabbed his collar with his last bit of strength, pulled him down to his face, and whispered into his ear. The grip became stronger around his neck, and the man could not break free from the soldier's grasp. He struggled to push himself away, but each time he released himself, the soldier reached out with the other hand. He struggled to stand, but found himself nose to nose with the dying young man. Suddenly, the soldier screamed.

~~~~~~

With the scream, Matt awoke with a start from his nightmare. His shirt was soaked, and perspiration dripped from his forehead and his palms. There was nothing he could do; he was in the throes of a full-blown panic attack now. Slowly he moved his gaze around his dark bedroom. He was thankful when he saw Duke's understanding eyes looking at him and felt the dog's reassuring paw being placed on his knee.

The next few minutes were going to be miserable, and Matt did what he could to lessen the impact of the onslaught of darkness. He closed his eyes and drew a deep breath through his nose. As he exhaled, he began to recite aloud, "The Lord is my shepherd: I shall not want. He maketh me to lie down in green pastures: he leadeth me beside the still waters."

Matt started to breathe heavier, yet shallower, and he struggled to continue the psalm. It was the only thing that had ever worked to ease the process, but tonight, the attack had started while he was asleep. He had no control over its beginning, which meant he would have little control over its finish. Still, he continued, "He restoreth my soul: he leadeth me in the paths of righteousness for His name's sake."

He was shaking now, and sharp pains moved like pinpricks up and down his arms and legs. Matt wrapped his arms around himself and sat on his bed, pulled up in a little ball. He rocked back and forth while burying his face into his knees. Duke laid his head on his paws as he stretched across the floor and fixed his sympathetic eyes on his loving master.

With the next words, came the tears: "Yea, though I walk through the valley of the shadow of death, I will fear no evil." At first, Matt's eyes simply filled with glossy moisture, but within seconds, large drops were forming and running down the sides of his face and off the tip of his nose. He tried to control the sadness, but every attempt he made to stop the emotions only sent him spiraling deeper into the abyss. He was gasping for breath through his loud sobbing, and he now yelled the next words of the Shepherd Psalm: "For thou art with me; thy rod and staff they comfort me."

He was spitting as he yelled the words, and now the sadness was being accompanied by anger. When he stood, his feet hit the cold, hard wood beside his bed with an abrupt thud. Duke jumped to his feet and took a couple of steps back. Matt put both his hands to his temples and pulled them backward over his sweat-drenched hair. As he pulled back, he fixed his gaze on the ceiling and yelled with all he could muster, *"I said, 'For thou art with me! Thy rod and staff they comfort me!' Where is my comfort?"*

Weak, he fell to his knees. He leaned forward and rested his elbows on the wood in front of him. Then Matt placed his forearms flat on the floor and pushed his forehead into his arms. He breathed in deeply through his mouth, allowing his back to arch, giving his lungs the full ability to expand and receive the surging volume of air. This time, he exhaled slowly through his nose.

Duke low-crawled the two feet separating him and Matt and placed himself on Matt's left side, touching the full length of his master's prostrated body on the floor. In a barely audible whisper, Matt continued, "Thou preparest a table before me in the presence of mine enemies: thou anointest my head with oil; my cup runneth over."

He snickered to himself. Duke acknowledged the new sound by raising his head and cocking it to one side. His ears moved up and down independently of each other, making him appear inquisitive and anticipatory for the changing mood. Matt remained on his knees and stretched out on his arms in front of him. He sniffed with nearly every breath and wiped his face against the sleeves of his now-soaked T-shirt. The room remained silent except for Matt's sniffles and Duke's panting.

Without raising his head, Matt reached over with his left hand and found Duke's left ear. He cupped the ear and scratched gently behind Duke's head. Cautiously, he raised his head and pulled his legs underneath him. Then he slowly turned and rested his back against the bed frame, extending his legs out in front of him. He stretched his neck by turning his head from side to side, closed his eyes, and leaned his head back until it lay flat on the mattress.

Duke stepped closer so Matt could reach him better. Matt instinctively reached out with his right hand and cradled Duke's face in both his hands. He picked his head up and placed his forehead on Duke's head and looked into his eyes. Softly, he whispered, "Surely goodness and mercy shall follow me all the days of my life: and I will dwell in the house of the Lord forever."

Chapter 2

The Blossom Dairy Diner sat on the edge of the city limits. It was a perfect location to cater to those folks going into town for business and others leaving town to work in the rail yard and the factory. The diner had started out of a Silver Stream trailer, and over the years, it had evolved into a single-story building with a glass window front. Most customers sat at the long, ivory-colored bar in chrome seats with sparkling red vinyl tops. But the few patrons who wanted conversation with their meal enjoyed the matching tables and chairs carefully positioned in the small area to the left of the bar.

Joe sat at one of the tables, looking out the diner's front windows. He was not able to sit with his back to the door. If something off kilter was going to happen, he was going to see it first. He sat tapping his watch and would only stop long enough to take long drinks from his mug of dark black coffee.

Naomi sat across from Joe and watched him look over her shoulder and out the windows. She would catch his eyes with a smile, and he would try to fashion his lips into a smile in return, but was only half successful. He would tap his watch a couple of times a bit harder, shake his head, and take another drink of coffee.

She reached across the table, placed her hand on Joe's, and patted it gently. "He is just running behind this morning, Joe," she said. "Don't worry. He will be here soon." No sooner had she finished the sentence, than a dark green pickup pulled up in front of the diner, and Joe could see Matt in the driver's seat. Joe sat up straight and stretched his shoulders by putting his hands on his lap and pushing down. At the top of the stretch, he gave a sigh of relief and said, "Finally, we can eat."

Matt looked in his rearview mirror as he put his newsboy hat on his balding head. His eyes were a little puffy and bloodshot to boot. But he was certain he could just pass it off as another sleepless night. Those are to be expected in the life of the clergy. Duke sat in the passenger's seat watching Matt looking at himself in the mirror. Drool formed in Duke's mouth as he smelled the aroma of bacon and sausage that permeated the air outside the diner. Matt straightened his hat and opened the door. He stepped out onto the gravel parking lot and was followed quickly by his faithful companion.

The bell rang as Matt opened the door to the restaurant, and he looked over at the familiar table where he met his friends every morning for breakfast. Originally, Wednesday was mandatory for them to get together, but over the years, most of the other days of the week had worked themselves into the schedule. Today was Thursday. Naomi turned and waved, Joe nodded, and Matt tipped his cap in reply.

He began to walk to the table, and Duke operated in stealth mode, low to the floor and eyes straight ahead. Duke went immediately under the table and lay down at Joe's feet. Matt smiled as he arrived at the table. "Duke, you traitor," he said with a laugh.

"Matt, I can't help it if your dog knows when he is in the presence of true class," Joe replied as he slipped a piece of freshly arrived bacon under the table to Duke. The dog was more than happy to accept the bribe.

Ignoring Joe's quip, Matt said, "Good morning, Naomi. I am sorry to have left you alone so long with this crotchety old coot.

Please accept my apologies." He shot a quick wink over at Joe and smiled. Joe shrugged his shoulder and waved his hand, and returned the smile.

Naomi enjoyed the banter between the two and tried to fuel the fire when she was able. "Well, I am glad you arrived when you did. Otherwise I would have to help Joe find a new crystal for his watch." Joe quickly put his hands under the table but jumped with a start and rapidly returned them to the surface when Duke surprised him by looking for more bacon. All three laughed.

"Matt," Joe began, "you look like you were on the losing end of a prizefight last night. What gives?"

"Joe!" Naomi admonished. "He hasn't even had his first sip of coffee yet."

"Aw, it's okay, Naomi. He is usually in such awe of my good looks that he can't handle it when I don't get my beauty sleep," Matt said playfully. "I have my weekly meeting with the Baron today," he continued with more seriousness, "and I never sleep well when I am preparing for those."

Joe nodded knowingly but stared hard at Matt to let him know he was not buying the explanation. Naomi quickly changed the subject. "Joe, tell him about Joseph's new position." Joe looked down at his plate of eggs and moved them with his fork. He had one arm draped over the chair beside him, and it seemed as if he became lost in the swirls his fork made in the bright yellow yolk on his plate.

Duke sighed underneath the table. The sigh seemed to bring Joe out of his trance, and he spoke, "Yeah, it seems Joseph has gotten a new job that pays next to nothing, living in the city where he can't help out his old man on the farm."

"Joe," Naomi admonished again. It was certainly not hard to see her foundations as an educator when she dealt with her two best friends. "You know it's a job to be proud of. He is helping out children. Now that is something precious."

"Spoken like a true teacher," Joe quipped. "Anyway, Matt, it seems as if he has gotten involved with some group that tries to help out inner-city kids who have a penchant for getting into trouble." He went back to stirring his eggs. "I don't know why I paid for four years of agricultural college for him to live in the city."

"Ah, Joe, he is helping out. There is something to be said about that," Matt offered in consolation.

"Spoken like a true preacher," Joe replied.

The three sat in silence for a while as they ate their breakfasts. Joe and Matt took turns slipping bacon, sausage, and pieces of biscuits under the table to Duke. Travelers were always shocked to see a dog in the diner, but most folks were quick to cover for Matt and Duke. "He has trouble with his eyesight," they would explain.

The passersby would nod in silent understanding. It was probably not such a good idea to lie about such a malady, especially with regard to the town reverend, but it usually put a quick end to the conversation and alleviated whatever concerns others may have had.

Naomi began telling a story of a young man in the current class she was instructing. The young man, "an exemplary student," as she stated it, was being forced to make the decision to decide between his education and the factory. He was a third-generation ironworker, and his family needed him to earn money, not improve his intellect. After all, how much intellect does a third-generation ironworker need? The two men shook their heads as Naomi continued with her tale. Unfortunately, the story she was recounting was all too familiar in this town.

During World War II, the government had built a large munitions factory just outside of the small town, comprised up to that point of cotton farmers. With the construction of the factory came the laying of railroad tracks so the munitions could be shipped to each coast quickly in an effort to replenish the quickly depleted stock of weapons. When the war ended, the munitions factory was no longer required. The operation was sold to a private business owner, Jesse Barrister, or as he had come to be known, "The Baron."

The lines in the factory could easily be changed to make various mechanical devices from car parts to toys. The central Texas location and the expansive network of railways made the list of customers long and varied for Barrister Enterprises. In the fifteen years since the war had ended, the Baron had converted the entire town into his business, and every citizen was his employee.

He owned the schools, the real estate, the hospital, and the church. If the young man in Naomi's class was going to drop out to work in the factory, she would receive no help from her administrators. The boy was doing exactly what the Baron wanted him to do.

As Naomi paused to take a sip of coffee, Joe raised his head to get a better vantage of the scene outside the diner. An 18-wheeler had just pulled up into the parking lot, and the truck jerked to a stop, then it jumped forward, only to jerk to another stop. Matt and Naomi, along with everyone else in the Blossom Dairy Diner, turned to watch the spectacle unfold.

The passenger door on the cab of the truck flew open, and a young girl jumped out, bypassing the steps altogether. Her cowboy boots hit the ground hard, and she nearly lost her balance on the uneven gravel surface. Her face became contorted as she realized she had left something in the cab of the truck. She jumped up on the rail and reached into the cab.

Just then the driver came around and grabbed her from behind. No sooner had he grabbed her than she came down on top of his head with a large, green canvas bag. From the way he reacted, she must have had bricks in that bag, because he immediately let go of her legs and cradled his head in his hands.

Again the girl jumped down from the cab, and this time darted, bag in hand, to the door of the diner. The driver, having shaken off the effects of the blow to the head, followed quickly behind her. She pulled open the door so hard that the bell nearly was pulled off its decorative metal resting spot. With haste, she stepped inside, threw her bag over her shoulder, and pulled the door shut. She put both feet against the doorjamb, grabbed the crossbar on the door, and pulled toward her with all her might.

The driver reached the door within seconds and began to pull at the door while yelling obscenities at her through the glass. Finally the young girl spoke. "Someone help me," she shouted. "He is crazy!" Everyone sat over their half-eaten plates of food and stared at the girl with open mouths.

Joe looked over at Matt. "Well, Preacher, looks like someone might need saving." Matt took a deep breath, pushed his chair back from the table, and stood.

Chapter 3

The driver pulled hard on the door and overpowered the young girl's grip. The door swung open, and as the bell rang, he grabbed the girl by the arm, causing her to drop her bag to the ground. Some of the contents spilled out along the cracked sidewalk, making various sounds of metal, plastic, and who knows what else.

The brief distraction was enough for the girl to lunge toward the closing diner door with her free arm. She caught the handle with her fingertips, and the door flung open as the lumberjack-looking fella spun her around. The big man looked up and in the center of the open doorway stood Matt, sipping on his cup of coffee.

Of course, Duke stood firmly between Matt's legs with his eyes keenly focused on the gruff man. Matt finished his sip, smacked his lips, and asked in a voice loud enough to get the attention of the duo, "So, what seems to be the problem here?"

"Nothing of your concern!" barked the driver.

"Seems to me you are hurting the girl," Matt retorted. "Now, that is my concern."

The angry man tightened his grip on the girl's arm and pushed her toward the door. Obviously he had forgotten he was trying to pull her away from the diner. But now he was engaged with a different foe—a foe who did not appear to be much of a challenge, but he would enjoy the opportunity for the collateral damage.

"Look, mister. This is not your business. Not your concern. So, I suggest you and your mutt go back to your breakfast before I send you both back with your tails between your legs."

"No thanks," replied Matt. "I am enjoying my coffee right here."

The girl was not screaming, but her face was contorted in pain. The lumberjack's grip was too much for her and, though she was a fighter, it was obvious she was close to her breaking point.

"Let the girl go. C'mon inside and have some breakfast yourself. Does she owe you money? I'll buy your meal and a bagged lunch. How's that sound? That should square everything up."

"Not hardly!" blurted the man, so angry that saliva foamed on the corners of his mouth. "That ain't what she owes me!"

"Then please, dear sir, tell all of these people in this establishment what you are expecting from this young girl, if not breakfast and a bagged lunch. We are all ears."

The driver looked around the diner. All eyes were fixed on him and awaiting his response. He swallowed hard, knowing that he had just lost this hand of poker. His gaze moved from left to right and back to the center, where it fell hard on Matt. He threw the girl down on the pavement, and she landed by her belongings. Immediately she grabbed her wrist, thankful to be free but still wincing from the pain. The man raised his right hand and balled it into a fist as he stepped toward Matt.

A shout came from someone in the diner, "No! He's blind!" There were visitors in the Blossom Dairy today. The shout threw the burly man's timing off, and he was surprised when Joe caught his arm in its swinging motion. During the commotion, Joe had worked his way to the side of the door and had been waiting for the man's move on Matt.

Joe turned the man's arm behind his back, just as the lumberjack had done to the girl, and directed him to his truck.

His feet scooted across the gravel, kicking up dust and pebbles. Duke encouraged the man's movement by barking at him every time he resisted the forward progress. Obscenities flew out of the man's mouth with each breath he took. Joe used all of his might to lock the man's arm and continue the forward push.

Matt turned back toward the counter where the waitress, Mary, sat a container full of eggs, potatoes, biscuits, and gravy. Beside it was a large cup of coffee, and another bag that contained some sort of sandwich and likely potato salad. Matt picked up the items, nodded at Mary, and headed outside. Naomi tended to the girl outside the diner as Matt walked past them to deliver his bagged goods.

Joe had successfully maneuvered the lumberjack back to his truck. They stood outside his cab, discussing the next phase of this encounter. "Now, I am going to let you go," said Joe. "I know you're mad, but you have to understand, this is over. It is time for you to move along. Do you understand that?"

The man tried to pull away, but Joe was locked in. There was no way out. Defeated, the man looked toward the sky and with a sigh, nodded in the affirmative. As Joe prepared to let go, the sheriff's car pulled up behind the men. "Everything okay here?" asked the deputy.

"Yep," replied Matt, "this fella was just picking up a to-go order, so Joe, Duke, and I brought it out to him." Matt handed the truck driver his food and cup of coffee and nodded. The man looked at Matt and Joe, then at the deputy, and climbed up into his cab and started the engine.

Matt, Joe, and Duke walked back to the diner. Joe rubbed his shoulder. Matt pulled a handkerchief from his pocket and wiped the back of his neck.

"Joe?"

"Yeah, Matt."

"What would you have done if the sheriff wouldn't have happened by?"

"Don't know, Matt ... hadn't thought it out that far. I imagine I would have taken a whuppin'," he said, realizing his good fortune.

Matt shook his head, and both men laughed. He patted Joe on the back as they walked back into the restaurant. Joe rubbed his arm and shoulder on the way. Duke led the two into the diner as they were all greeted with applause and the sound of imitation silverware on cheap glass. Both men held sly grins as they headed back to their table. There, Naomi sat with the young girl.

Chapter 4

Matt and Joe waved and shook the hands of other customers as the two walked to their seats. It was as if they were running for political office and were the candidates to beat. But they were quickly given a reality check by Naomi as they approached the table.

"Matt, is that any way for a preacher to behave? And Joe, why whatever were you thinking? That fella was twice your size and half your age. Next time, you boys wait for help. You are not twenty anymore!" Both men looked down at the floor. Even Duke hung his head.

After what seemed the appropriate amount of time for repentance, Matt sat down and grabbed a piece of bacon. "And whom do we have the pleasure of dining with this morning?"

His eyes were fixed on the young girl sitting across the table from him. She was possibly seventeen years old, but likely younger. The blue-jean jacket she wore was torn and tattered, and her jeans fit the same description. The boots she wore on the outside of her jeans were ornate and had a cross with angel wings embroidered on each one.

The girl tapped the heels of the beautiful boots repeatedly as she nervously shook her legs. Her hair was brown and long, and it obscured the view of her face as she sat with her head down. But from what could be seen, her face looked tired, sad, and scared. She sat in silence and did not answer Matt.

David C. Hall

Mary came to the table and asked the young lady if she would like anything. The girl did not look at Mary, but she muttered, almost in a whisper, "Water." Joe shook his head and gave a look to Mary, Matt, and Naomi that let them know this was as absurd a situation as he had ever been in.

"Mary," said Joe, "please bring the young lady some toast, eggs, and bacon. Thaw out some of that fresh-squeezed orange juice for her too. While you're at it, I will take some sausage links. That fella's daggone dog ate all mine." Mary smiled, winked at Matt, and left to fill the order.

"Now listen here, young lady." Joe turned his focus on the girl beside him. "You came into this place causing quite a ruckus, so don't be acting all shy now. I believe we have earned the right to know your name and whatever story you want to make up about Paul Bunyan out there."

"Oh, Joe," Naomi said, shaking her head.

"What?" Joe replied with his hands raised in innocence.

Naomi started, "Please forgive my cranky old friend—"

"My name is Sarah," the young girl interrupted. The three friends looked at each other, then at her.

Slowly Sarah raised her head and looked at Matt. "Thank you for helping me," she said, and offering a quick glance at Joe, added, "both of you. I don't have any money for food, so I will just drink my water. As for that fat jerk out there, well he was my ride to Mexico. He had other plans though."

Mary returned with the food, and the sound of the plates being set on the table brought Duke to his feet underneath. They all sat in silence for a moment. "Water?" Joe finally questioned. "Eat some breakfast. It is Matt's turn to buy anyway."

Matt sipped gingerly at his hot coffee and watched the girl attack her plate of breakfast food like she was a grizzly at a sushi bar. She paused every few bites and rubbed her belly.

16

He stole glances at Naomi and Joe, both returning smiles and nods.

Matt set his mug on the table and leaned forward on both arms. "Sarah, do you have any idea what you will do now?"

She stopped eating and looked at him. He could tell she was sizing him up. Indeed she was. Sure he had come to her aid, which made him quite chivalrous. But there was something else she could see in his eyes. Something she identified with. It comforted and scared her at the same time. She made her reply short and to the point: "I am going to Mexico."

"Well, not today you're not," Matt replied. "Naomi has an extra room at her place where you will bunk tonight. You need a good night's rest and, if you don't mind me saying it, a shower."

"Thanks for bringing that up," Joe added.

"Naomi is teaching a class this morning, so you are going to have to drive over to the church with me and spend time there until this afternoon. That is, unless you want to go work in the fields with Joe."

"Mister," Sarah said with her voice raised, "I don't have to follow you, and I don't have to stay anywhere where I don't want."

"True, young lady," Naomi replied, "but getting to Mexico from the middle of Texas with no money doesn't sound like the simplest of journeys. You best just take the day to figure out your plan, and then you can leave in the morning."

Sarah sat looking at Naomi with her mouth poised for a retort, but she was unable to speak. She glanced at Matt, who smiled; then at Joe, who shrugged; then back at Naomi, who folded her hands on the table and held her head high in a triumphant posture.

Sarah looked at Naomi, then with more sincerity than she had carried on the rest of her conversation simply stated, "But you don't know me."

Matt took a drink of his coffee and set the mug on the table. His eyes watched the coffee ripple inside the mug for just a moment. Then he raised his eyes, pointed at the girl with his mug, and said, "Sure we do. You are Sarah."

Chapter 5

Sarah spent a good ten minutes resisting the offers of help from Matt and Naomi, but in the end, she knew they were right and that she was truly between the proverbial rock and a hard place. Although the food was very much needed, it was also making her feel somewhat nauseous.

Not only was she feeling out of sorts, but the lumberjack had taken her purse before their scuffle and, with it, most of her money. She still had a little tucked in the heel of her boot, but it was not nearly enough to get her to Mexico. Even more importantly, it was not enough for her to conduct the business she needed to while there. She was going to have to bide her time and figure out a way to get more funds. However, the clock was ticking, and she could not hang around this godforsaken town for too long.

Matt gave Naomi a hug and put his hands on her shoulders. "We will catch up with you after school lets out. You don't take any flak from those political types over there." He looked over at Joe, who was stealing the last piece of bacon from the plate as he stood. "Joe." Matt grabbed the brim of his hat and nodded.

"Matt," Joe said with half a piece of bacon hanging from his mouth and two fingers raised to his temple in a quasisalute.

"I will see you in a bit, Sarah," said Naomi. "It was nice sharing breakfast with you." Sarah smiled crookedly, then looked down.

"Sarah, you keep that old dog in line. He is always getting into trouble if we aren't around to hold his leash," Joe said. "Watch out for Duke too," he added with a grin. Sarah partly smiled, but didn't raise her head.

Matt walked to the passenger side of his truck and opened the door. Duke jumped up into the truck first and moved to the center of the seat, inviting Sarah to sit next to him. Matt threw Sarah's duffle bag in the bed of his truck, and she hopped into the seat next to Duke. Matt walked around the front of the truck, opened his door, and grabbed the wheel to pull himself in.

Sarah looked closely at this man, whom she had found herself in the company of. He was older, but not old, she thought. Maybe around fifty or older, would be her guess. She thought Naomi and Joe were around the same age. Matt was cleanly shaven, but he had missed a section on his neck under his chin. The majority of the whiskers she could see were gray. He was a handsome man, although he was no Paul Newman. He looked very tired though, and his handsome features were accented with darkening circles beneath his eyes and worry lines across his forehead. She thought that he would make a good grandfather though. He looked the part.

Matt started the truck and patted Duke on the head as he backed out of his spot. He turned out of the gravel parking lot onto Main Street, and they began the very short trip to the church only a few blocks away. He looked at Sarah and smiled. Then he focused his attention back on the road. It was odd, because Sarah had expected a lecture from him. She had been around preachers or folks who called themselves Christians many times. They usually had a lot to say about the way she lived her life, the choices she made, and the amount of repentance she should be accomplishing. So, Matt's silence was a surprise to her and, in a way, made her uneasy.

They pulled into a parking space that had a sign that read, "Main Street Chapel: Preacher." Matt looked at Sarah and nodded toward the sign. "I am kind of a big deal around here." He laughed at his own joke. Sarah and Duke looked at each other as if to say, "Oh, brother." Sarah climbed out the passenger door and held it open for Duke, but he had already bounded out the driver's side door and was making his way up the brick walkway toward the church doors.

Matt let Sarah know her bag would be fine in the truck. She, on the other hand, thought differently and insisted on carrying the big, green bag. Matt held his hand out inviting her to follow Duke up the walkway.

As a rule, Sarah avoided churches and the people in them. But she had little choice now that she was here. She made her way to the door, and Matt followed behind. The church looked as if it was from a storybook. The building they were walking toward was attached to the main structure of the church. She discerned this by the presence of a beautiful steeple and a large, circular, stained-glass window facing the street on the other building. The single-story building they were ready to enter was covered in the same white wood siding, but the windows were plain and the roof was absent of a steeple.

Matt reached out and pulled the door open for Sarah and Duke. Duke went in first and quickly disappeared. Sarah stepped in and found herself in a long hallway or waiting room of sorts. There was a desk at the end of the room and chairs lined both walls. From around the corner, an African-American woman appeared and was shaking her head at Matt.

"You better get back there, Preacher. You are late!" she said as she took off his jacket and pushed him toward the hallway.

"Wow," said Matt. "We had some excitement this morning," he said, glancing at Sarah, "and I totally forgot."

"Well, *he* didn't," the lady said, still shaking her head and nudging Matt along.

Quickly he gestured at Sarah. "Albie, this is Sarah." Then gesturing at the lady, he continued, "Sarah, this is Albie." Albie and Sarah both looked at each other and nodded. "Albie, I was hoping you could take a look through the clothes closet with Sarah here and help her find some less-worn items."

Albie looked at the tattered denim covering Sarah's body. "Shouldn't be hard to do," she replied. "Now get going, Preacher," she urged. "You wait right there little lady," Albie said to Sarah while pointing at a chair beside the desk. "I will be right back. I have got to get the preacher his coffee. Lordy, he is going to need it."

Albie made her way to the entrance to a small kitchenette area, which Sarah could make out from where she was sitting. She could hear Albie preparing the coffee, but she also heard a sound like snoring. She looked around the corner and saw nothing, so she stood and looked over the desk back into the rest of the office. No one else was there. Yet she was certain she heard snoring from someone who was sound asleep.

Albie returned and said, "That is going to take a little bit to percolate, so how about a tour?" Sarah nodded and instinctively followed Albie as she started walking.

As they moved around the corner, Sarah glanced down and saw the source of the snoring. There lay Duke, sprawled across the floor under the desk. Albie snickered, "He has a bed in the preacher's office, but he doesn't care much for Mr. Barrister."

~~~⟋⟍⟋⟍⟋~~~

Matt took a deep breath and entered his office. It was not a big room, but it was nicely appointed with a Shaker-style desk and hutch flanked by matching bookshelves along the wall. Joe and Matt had worked together to make the set eons ago.

On the wall behind the desk was a painting of a bald eagle gliding over a snowcapped mountain, the sun was shining through the clouds and causing the eagle's wings to glisten. The writing on the bottom read, "Isaiah 40:31: For they that wait upon the Lord shall run and not be weary. They shall walk and not faint."

He reached over and placed his hat on the coatrack behind the door. The Baron stood with his back to Matt and pretended to be examining the painting with the discernment of an art dealer.

"Matt," he said without turning around, "this is a horrible picture. The light shines from all sorts of different angles, and that is either the biggest dang eagle I have ever seen or the mountain is a prairie dog mound on the plains of Texas."

"Well, Mr. Barrister," Matt replied as he took a seat in one of the two chairs facing the desk, "that is all a matter of perspective."

The Baron put his hands on his hips and turned around to face Matt, while shaking his head and exaggerating his smile. "I suppose many things are a matter of perspective, eh, Matt?"

"I suppose," he replied while scratching the back of his head.

Matt could tell he was about to receive one of the Baron's lectures on a topic of success, money, management, or some other fine business attribute. The Baron sat down in Matt's tall-back desk chair and moved some of the objects around on the desk. Picking up a nickel-plated letter opener, he crossed his legs and leaned back in the chair. He gripped the letter opener in his right hand between the thumb and index finger and pushed the point against the index finger of his left hand. He removed his left hand from the opener and waved the tool in the air like it was a sword.

The Baron smiled and snickered. His mostly gray mustache covered his upper lip so the evidence of the smile was his crooked teeth being visible to Matt as he looked on. "See, my dear Reverend, perspective is truly changed depending on which end of the sword you are facing."

Then he leaned forward on the desk with his hands flat against the wood and pulled his face closer to Matt's. "I make it a matter of policy to be the one on the operating end."

"Maybe I am missing something here, Mr. Barrister," said Matt. He stood and walked behind his seat, then he leaned on the back of the chair with both hands. Matt directed a sarcastic question to the man across the desk. "Are you challenging me to a duel?" The Baron did not laugh.

"Perspective, Reverend, is having a town pastor who does not get in fights at diners and then show up to meetings fifteen minutes late." The Baron tried to contain his anger as he made the statement.

"Depends once again on whose perspective," Matt responded with every bit the firmness that the Baron had maintained. "Mr. Barrister, I appreciate the funds you and your family provide the church, but this is a community establishment; it is not one of your private businesses." Matt knew he had crossed a line as soon as his retaliation was out of his mouth.

The Baron stood and stared hard at Matt. The two men locked eyes. Matt did not wish to be confrontational, but he found it hard to back down.

The Baron spoke firmly. "We both know you are wrong in your last statement, Matt. But you have had an eventful morning, so I will let it pass. I will, however, give you an admonishment; please remember who pays your salary, Reverend. It is not God."

The Baron nodded his head emphatically to acknowledge that the final point on the matter had been made. Matt walked around to the front of the chair and sat down gently, leaning forward with his hands folded in his lap. He looked at the Baron, and the Baron stared back smugly.

~~~⌒⌒⌒~~~

Albie walked Sarah through the maze of boxes in the back room. Many were marked as decorations; those that were not marked were covered in dust, indicating that whatever was in the box was not used and not missed. They passed a Nativity set that was quite large, Sarah thought, for a small church. The wise men were in a circle presenting their presents to each other, and Joseph, Mary, and the baby Jesus were wrapped in some type of plastic.

Albie made her way to the door on the other side of the storage area and dug through her pocket. "Oh, I know I have this key in here somewhere," she said. She pulled out gum, tissues, fingernail clippers, a paper clip, some plastic toy thing Sarah had never seen, then finally, the small padlock key she was looking for.

"Amen," said Albie. "Seek and ye shall find." She looked at Sarah with a big smile. After unlocking the padlock and opening the door, Albie walked into the dark room. There was click and a flicker of light as she pulled the string on the lightbulb overhead. Sarah looked through the doorway at several racks of clothes and shelves of shoes.

Albie walked past Sarah. "You start browsing, honey. I have to take the preacher his coffee … if he has even made it this long." With that, Albie was out of the door and hustling down the hallway.

Sarah walked slowly and ran her fingers over the top of the clothes hanging on the long racks. Many of the baby clothes still had the tags attached from the original purchase. She wrinkled her nose and shook her head as she thought about the extravagant life those people must lead …

~~~⌒⌒⌒~~~

The nursery held a beautiful white crib and two matching rocking chairs side by side. The mother opened the closet to reveal rows and rows of beautiful outfits as the father bounced the laughing baby on his knee. Together they prepared the baby for bed, and then they sat in the chairs. The mother rocked gently as the father read a bedtime story. Then the mother laid the baby in the crib beneath a mobile of butterflies, which the father wound. As a lullaby played, the parents kissed the child good-night and smiled as they walked arm in arm from the room …

~~∞∞∞~~

A clanking sound brought Sarah out of her daydream. It sounded as if it came from the wall on the side opposite from where she stood. She was more curious than frightened, so she made her way through the maze of racks and piles of clothes to the other side.

Once there, she found a bin pushed against the wall; it contained clothes of all types. There was a metal contraption above the bin that had an opening to the outside, and it was closed by a spring-loaded metal plate. When clothes were put through the slot, the plate would close automatically.

Sarah pulled down the plate and let go. It was not the sound she had heard. She moved to the other side of the chute and saw a different metal box. This one was completely closed. A metal chute attached to the wall traveled two feet down into a metal container. The metal container had a door that was closed and locked with a small padlock. To Sarah, it looked like the padlock did little to guard the contents and served more to keep the door shut.

As she examined this, she heard movement at the top of the chute, the mutter of people talking, a rush of air into the chute, followed by the sound of change being dropped through the opening and landing in the container below. The sound created by the landing donation showed that the container was quite full of change already. Sarah's eyes widened.

~~~~

Matt opened his mouth to speak but was interrupted by a knock at the door, then a twisting of the handle. Albie walked in with two coffee mugs. "Excuse me, Preacher, but here is your coffee. Mr. Barrister, I took to making you a cup too, but didn't know your liking of cream and sugar." She dug into her pocket and pulled out some creamer packs and sugar cubes, then set them on the desk by Mr. Barrister's coffee cup. He said nothing and looked away as she tried to make eye contact.

Albie turned toward Matt and rolled her eyes. Matt inhaled deeply through his nose as he savored the aroma of the coffee, and then he took a small drink of the hot, black liquid. He closed his eyes and smiled. "Thank you, Miss Albie, this is the finest coffee in town."

Albie cracked a smile as she walked out of the room. She glanced at Matt as she shut the door behind her, and he heard her say, "Mmmmm-huh," as she walked away.

As soon as the sound of the latch catching on the door could be heard, Mr. Barrister pushed the coffee cup away and started into Matt. "Let's return to the topic of perspective, Matt," he said agitatedly. "You can have anyone in the church as your secretary, but you choose to hire a colored woman. How do you think that makes our church look? What perspective does that provide? Now, I know she is nice enough, but if we want to get people in the pews on Sunday, we cannot divide the congregation."

Matt took a drink of his coffee and looked over the brim of his cup at Mr. Barrister. "Jesse, technically, this is God's house — regardless of who pays my salary—and here we are all on equal ground." The use of Mr. Barrister's surname was not an oversight, but an exclamation mark to his point. Mr. Barrister frowned as he realized the implication.

"Do you think people come to this church based on their faith, *Matt*?" He emphasized Matt's name to return the favor. Matt did not have a chance to answer. "They come here because they do not want to work on the Sunday shift, and they know I will give them the time off to attend services. If I don't see them in service, well, they may find themselves running some equipment the following weekend."

He pulled the coffee cup on the desk back toward him, opened the creamer packet, and poured the contents in the cup, followed by a sugar cube. The Baron was perplexed for a moment as he realized he had nothing to stir the coffee with, but then laid his eyes on the letter opener. He picked up the opener and dipped it in his coffee, stirring the contents.

"Let's face it, Reverend," he continued, "God is not the foundation of this town. That distinction belongs to Barrister Enterprises. I offer my employees the illusion of the American dream, and you help me to complete that illusion by standing in the pulpit of the little white church."

Matt focused a steely glare on the Baron. There were so many words and verses running through his mind—he had no idea what he would utter first. The man sitting in front of him thought of himself as greater than the Almighty, and there was nothing Matt wanted to do more than to knock him down off the pedestal. The Baron sat in the chair with an audacious smirk on his face as he waited for Matt's response. Matt's body had not fully recovered from its ordeal of the previous night, and he felt shaky and mentally foggy. And added to that, his palms were beginning to perspire.

Mustering all the composure he was able, Matt replied, "You place yourself in high regard, Jesse. I would suggest you take a look at Proverbs 16:18. I am sure that verse will have great meaning for you." Mr. Barrister did not like Matt using his proper name, but decided to let it go.

"Matt, you stick to the preaching and the Bible reading. I will stick to running this town." Then, seemingly happy with the outcome of this morning's war of words, Mr. Barrister reached into his coat pocket and pulled out a cigar. He reached into his front pocket, retrieved a clip, snipped the end, and placed the cigar between his teeth. Through his clenched teeth he asked Matt, "So, what is your sermon on this week?"

~~∞∞~~

Sarah stared at the box containing the donations. She figured one hard pull of the padlock would loosen the grip it had on the door. Once accomplished, the contents would be hers, and she could move on. She looked over her shoulder, then closed her eyes and listened for footsteps. Hearing nothing except the air from the outside moving in through the slots in the wall, Sarah reached for the lock, then pulled her hands back quickly. She realized there was no way for her to carry her loot, even if she was able to open the door.

So she stood and looked around the room. On the far wall there were handbags of all types. She made her way back across the room and examined the bags. Just then Albie walked into the room. "My girl, don't you know you pick out the outfit first, *then* you can accessorize." Sarah flashed a nervous grin.

~~∞∞~~

Matt knew the question was coming. This was the typical format for their weekly meetings. It began with a challenge, followed by a puffing of the chest, then a lighting of a cigar, followed by the topic of the sermon. Matt was happy this was the last act in the song and dance.

"I have planned a nice discussion on faith centered on the parable of the mustard seed," Matt said as he looked at the bottom of his empty coffee mug.

"Well, that won't do," admonished Mr. Barrister. "The employees at the plant are slipping on their numbers; too complacent, if you ask me. I need you to repeat that sermon you gave about working for me like they are working for God." His face bore a proud look as he recalled the comparison he had just made.

"We just had that sermon two weeks ago!" Matt retorted.

"Obviously no one listened to you, Reverend. The numbers have not improved," the Baron stated quickly and matter of factly. He pulled the cigar from between his teeth and held it between his forefinger and long finger, then pointed it at Matt's chest.

"Give the sermon again, Matt, or I'll find someone who will." The Baron placed the cigar back in his mouth, stood, and made his way to the door. He looked back at Matt as he opened the door. Matt was staring at the eagle soaring high above the mountain in the painting behind his desk.

Just before he shut the door, the Baron leaned back over his shoulder and asked, "How's that for perspective?" Matt let out a sigh as the door slammed.

Chapter 6

Central High School was typical of most industrial towns. The classes taught were primarily vocational in their instruction. There were various manufacturing labs that contained different configurations for processing. These configurations were all replicas of the Barrister Plant and donated by none other than Jesse Barrister himself. Of course, the science laboratories were highly maintained, the gymnasium was stocked with equipment, and the most recent textbooks were available to the students at no cost; all done by the courtesy of Barrister Enterprises.

The school was part of the county board of education, but because of its strong private support, it was granted certain leniencies. For instance, at the age of sixteen, students were allowed to apprentice at the Barrister Plant for half a day for school credit. Often this credit was applied to mathematics or the sciences, allowing the student to spend more time mastering the vocation of his or her choice in the labs.

Naomi taught English at Central High School, and she was completing her last week of classes prior to summer break. This week would mark the end of over thirty years of teaching. She did not expect many of her students to be in class today. With only two days left, most had caught the summer bug and were meeting at the old rock quarry for a swim and whatever else teenagers did.

She was hoping to have one last discussion of *A Farewell to Arms* before the summer though. It was one of her favorite books and, with the current conditions facing the world, she thought it would be beneficial for the younger generation to hear Hemingway's account of the front lines of World War I.

She took out her book and thumbed through its pages. There were some notes she had prepared for the discussion, so she reached into her bag and retrieved a black composition book and opened it to her last entry. Naomi had many of these composition books, and it was likely that ten of them contained the same notes she now read. But she found it fresh and exciting to revisit the text each year.

Her door opened, and three students walked into her class. Two of these students she expected, but she was surprised and excited to see the third. Danny and Susan were vying for the valedictorian of the graduating class, so each of them was working to find that edge that would tip the scale in his or her favor. But Peter, he was likely expected by his friends at the quarry. Yet, he was in class with Hemingway's book in his hand. Peter was the boy she had spoken about to Matt and Joe earlier that morning.

"Well, good morning, my friends," Naomi said with a smile. "I must say I was expecting to have the Hemingway discussion with myself this morning." The students laughed a little at the remark. After all, regardless of their motives, they were still teenagers and would rather be someplace else than a classroom.

"Okay, honestly now, did you guys actually read the book?" Naomi expected hands to be half raised and a look that said they had not finished the novel. However, all three nodded their heads energetically and replied in the affirmative.

Peter pounced on the opportunity to ask the question that must have bothered him since he read the last sentence in the book. "What did he do?"

Naomi looked quizzically at Peter. "What did who do?"

"Lieutenant Henry," replied Peter. "I mean, where did he go? Did he stay in Switzerland? Did he return to fighting? What happened to him?" The other two students looked back and forth between their friend Peter and their instructor.

Naomi fought the tears welling up in her eye, for she knew the problem that Peter was having. In Hemingway's novel, Lieutenant Henry and Nurse Barkley had dreams and desires for their lives. They were very much in love and in, what seemed to be, a perpetual state of bliss, even during a war. Yet, reality can only be avoided for so long. Eventually the workings of the world and its sometimes cruel reality can crush dreams with a heavy hand. It is a hard lesson to learn, and Hemingway's narrative punches the reader in the gut with an unpleasant example.

Peter, Naomi surmised, was realizing that his dreams and hopes were likely not the reality the world had planned for him. He wanted to be told that such a scenario was merely a work of fiction. But the innocence was gone; he knew the truth: reality can hurt.

"Those are questions the reader is left with, Peter," replied Naomi. "Lieutenant Henry leaves the hospital and enters a life of uncertainty. Every plan and every idea has been wiped clean. What does he have to hold on to?" asked Naomi. "Does he have hope? In fact, does his character ever have hope in the reality of the world in which he lives?"

The three students sat still, thumbing through their books, searching for answers to their teacher's questions. Finding a relevant part of the text, Susan responded, "I don't know that he has hope, but I think he believes in something greater ... I am not sure he has much faith in it though."

"What do you mean by that?" Peter asked before Naomi had the chance.

"I think because he defends the priest and enjoys the priest's company, but does not really practice the religion, it shows he is not against believing that there is something more to life." Susan looked at Naomi for approval.

"That is a great observation," Naomi assured Susan, then continued to explain. "I think what Susan is sharing is a hint to the reader that Lieutenant Henry wants to believe in something greater than himself. We could argue that it is the proper cause for war—his love for Nurse Barkley, or even God." She searched for eye contact to ensure they were following her. "But, for some reason, he always stops short of trusting his inclination to believe in something. He deserts his cause, keeps the priest at a distance, and loses his love."

She paused, allowing them to soak in her analysis, then posed Peter's question a bit differently: "What does that mean for Lieutenant Henry at the end of the book?"

"I think he is indifferent," said Danny. "He has pretty much lost everything, and he is alone in a place that is unfamiliar. He is numb; he is indifferent to reality. He probably doesn't care." They all sat in silence for a moment.

Curse you, Ernest Hemingway, Naomi thought to herself.

Peter broke the silence. "It was not what I was expecting, is all." He flipped through his books and thought aloud. "They had been through so much and were finally going to be happy."

Danny cleared his throat a little bit and shifted in his seat as he seemed to be considering his next words carefully. Finally he asked, "Were they really going to be happy though?"

Before the others had the chance to respond, he continued, "Lieutenant Henry was AWOL, war was still raging, money was being supplied by Lieutenant Henry's estranged family, they were not married, and neither seemed terribly happy about starting a family. It was if they were just pretending the whole time anyway.

"So, reality wasn't a surprise because it had always been known. Both knew there was no happy ending to their story. Even Hemingway clues the reader in throughout the book that this is the case." Susan and Peter looked at Danny with at first disagreement, then with understanding.

Naomi folded her hands on her desk and looked down at the notes she had prepared for this discussion. In a soft voice she began, "In my planned discussion for this class, we would have concentrated on Hemingway's use of terse sentences and abrupt dialogue to tell his story. We would have taken a look at examples of his description of trench warfare and the confusion of the front lines during World War I. These are the items that make this book academically interesting." She paused and rose from her desk.

Naomi found a connection with each of the three students who sat before her. "But you, my wonderful friends, have gone deeper than my notes allowed. You have opened up topics of duty, reality, love, and religion. You have supposed the question as to whether or not we are capable of changing a predetermined outcome. From your responses and melancholy, I think you believe that Lieutenant Henry and Nurse Barkley's relationship was ill-fated from the beginning, and that it could not be changed."

She pulled a chair out from behind an empty desk, spun it around, and sat as close to her students as she could. "But you also talked about belief and faith. Did Lieutenant Henry or Nurse Barkley really ever have faith or believe that things were going to turn out differently? Did they trust in their own happy ending?

"Think about that, and as you do, please realize that I have belief in each of your abilities to succeed in all you do. I have faith that you will continue to push yourselves to use those abilities to your highest potential." Each of the students looked at Naomi and felt a surge of pride by her encouragement. Peter's eyes met hers for a moment then looked away.

Naomi excused the students from the class. She stood by the door as the students exited into the hallway. Susan stopped and wrapped her arms around Naomi in a tight embrace. She did not say a word as Naomi returned her embrace, then the teacher grabbed Susan's shoulder and pushed her back a bit.

With Naomi's hands still on her shoulders, she looked at Susan and gave a reassuring nod. Susan smiled and stepped into the hallway. As Naomi turned, Danny stood in front of her with his outstretched hand. Naomi grabbed Danny's hand in a firm handshake. They both laughed at the seriousness of the exchange. Then Danny followed Susan into the hallway.

Peter looked at the floor as Naomi reached for his hand. She took his hand between both of hers, and he raised his eyes. "Peter," she said, "our reality is what we make it." Peter nodded.

Almost in a whisper, he responded, "I was accepted to the university." Naomi's eyes welled with tears. He continued, "My father doesn't know yet, but I will tell him soon. Thank you for believing in me." He smiled at her and gave her a quick hug. As he turned to leave, Naomi slapped him on the back and laughed.

She followed her students through the doorway and looked proudly down the heavily waxed hallway as three young people strode confidently and triumphantly into their promising futures.

Chapter 7

Matt opened the door to his office and found Duke sitting directly in front of him. "Coward," Matt said, shaking his head. Duke dropped his head and looked at Matt with the saddest eyes he could make.

Bending down on one knee, he placed his hand under Duke's chin. "No worries, boy. I would hide too." He scratched Duke's head and rose to his feet.

The two walked down the hall to the reception area where they found Albie and Sarah talking in the break room. The two had been engrossed in conversation but quieted as soon as Matt walked in the room. Sarah sat at a round table with two stacks of neatly folded clothes in front of her.

Motioning toward the clothes, Matt remarked, "Better than a regular ole Macy and Gimble's, huh?"

Albie laughed, "Yes sirree. She has a whole new wardrobe, and it even includes a dress or two."

Looking at Sarah, Matt offered, "Well, every young lady should have a dress or two." Sarah smiled but said nothing.

Albie examined Matt for a moment. He looked tired. "The Baron in a good mood this morning?" she asked.

"Yeah," Matt replied, "I think he did smile once or twice." He made his way to the coffeepot and poured himself another half-cup of coffee. His sleepless night was starting to catch up with him. Matt felt a little shaky, and his palms were becoming moist with perspiration. He looked into his coffee cup and briefly saw the face of a crying soldier.

Quickly he took a drink and turned to Sarah. "Well, I suppose we should take you to the supermarket to get you the items you need for your trip."

"Trip?" Albie asked.

"Yep," Matt said. "Didn't Sarah tell you? She is headed to Mexico."

~~~∞∞∞~~~

Joe took the wrench and threw it to the ground in exasperation. The tractor he used had been handed down to him from his father, and it had been used even before his father bought it. Changing the attachments was a two-man job, and Joe was alone. Previously he had several hands on the farm helping him, but two bad crops had put his operating budget deeply into the red.

He reached into the pocket on his bib overalls and pulled out his pipe. It was a beautiful piece of work, and he admired it every time he pulled it out of hiding. As he unfolded the handkerchief that covered the pipe, he could see the deep red textures of the cherrywood and the fine, dark lines of the highly polished grain. It made him smile instantly. He had been carrying the pipe for over twenty years, and its beauty was only surpassed by the story behind his acquisition of the fine cherry smoker.

Reaching into his back pocket, Joe removed a bag of cherry tobacco and dipped the pipe into the bag. Sufficiently packed, he removed the pipe, folded and replaced the bag, and put the pipe to his lips. A flick of his butane lighter ignited a flame that he used to light the pleasant-smelling tobacco. He perched himself on the seat of his tractor and took a couple of long puffs on the pipe. He closed his eyes for a moment as he fell into memories triggered by the aroma of the tobacco and the pipe in his hand.

Opening his eyes, he looked out over his fields of cotton. So far the crop seemed to be doing well. There were no blooms yet, but they were still a couple of weeks from expecting to see that type of growth. Yet, the plants on the eighty acres of Joe's farm seemed to remind him that his farm was dying. He had taken out a loan on the farm to plant the crop this season. It was his last-ditch effort to save the farm for his son, Joseph.

Only, Joseph had let him know, just yesterday, that he was not interested in running the family business. He was striking out on his own. Now, Joe realized how truly alone he was. He closed his eyes again and concentrated on the rich aroma of the cherry tobacco trying to drift away to those pleasant memories of the past.

He was startled out of his daydreams by the sound of a car coming up the driveway. He could not make out the car, only the location indicated by the blowing dirt and the dust that trailed behind the automobile. Somewhat perturbed to be interrupted from his break, he removed his hat and pulled out his work handkerchief to wipe his neck and face.

Placing the handkerchief back in his hat, and his hat back on his head, he stepped down from the tractor and moved toward the driveway. He walked slowly so he could savor the remaining tobacco in his pipe. Joe rounded the corner of the house, and there walking toward him was his son.

~∾∾∾∾~

Matt, Sarah, and Duke walked out of the church and across the square toward the local market. "I really don't need anything," Sarah insisted.

"At the very least you need a toothbrush and toothpaste. Everyone needs those two items before traveling," Matt replied. "By the way," he continued, "I don't recall why you were going to Mexico." He made no glances or facial expressions that would suggest that he knew she had not volunteered the information to the group this morning.

"I don't recall telling you," Sarah replied.

"Oh, I thought you had mentioned something." Matt shrugged his shoulders. "In that case," he continued, "why are you going?"

Sarah stopped walking and stared hard at Matt. "Let's just say I am going down to look for lost souls," she said angrily.

"Funny," Matt said calmly, "that's my job."

~∽⌒⌒∽~

Joseph walked up to his father with his hand outstretched. "Hello, Dad." Joe picked up his pace and met his son's outstretched hand with his own.

He slapped his son on the shoulder and stated, "Well, Joseph, this is a great surprise." Joe looked at his son, and he saw a younger, fitter, better version of himself. His hair was long, but combed. He wore a T-shirt and still preferred his cowboy boots beneath his jeans. He was tall and lean, but muscular. He looked like a man, but Joe still saw a boy.

When World War II began, Joe's wife, Annie, was already pregnant with Joseph. It was a different time then, and folks were called to duty quickly. Joe and Matt decided to join the effort early on, and unfortunately, Joe did not know about Annie's condition when he signed on the dotted line. With an expectant wife, he shipped out for basic training and God-only-knew what else.

Little did he know he would be returning in seven months to hold his newborn son and bury his wife. Thank God for his sister-in-law, as he would have never made it through the war without her caring for Joseph. In some respects, he returned to battle thinking it would be better for them all if he perished, but he did not, and now twenty years later, here he stood with his son.

"Do you want a sandwich or something?" asked Joe.

"Sure. That would be great. What do you have?" Joseph replied with a smile.

Together they both exclaimed, "Fried hot bologna." Laughing, they opened the screen door and stepped into the small house on the large farm, where together, they had coped with the loss of a mother and a wife.

"Dad," Joseph began as Joe sliced bologna in large, half-inch slices, "I couldn't just let our conversation end the way it did yesterday. I know you're disappointed." Joe said nothing, but continued to prep the bologna for the sandwiches. He moved to the stove and removed a large iron skillet from a hook above the stove.

Joseph continued, "There is just a need for people to help these kids who are so lost, Dad. Don't you understand? I felt so lost for so long, and I had you all. Can you imagine how hard it is for the kids who don't have anyone?" Joe cut four slits in each of the slices of bologna and placed each slice into the bubbling butter in the skillet, but said nothing.

"This is where I am needed, Dad. It is where God wants me. I don't want to disappoint you; I want you to understand and give me your blessing."

Throwing his head back, Joe looked at the ceiling. He focused on the coffee stain above the stove, a result of a percolator mishap. Joseph used his foot to slide out one of the chairs at the kitchen table, and he sat firmly in the seat.

Joe closed his eyes and exhaled deeply. "Son," he finally replied, "I have prepared you from the day you were born to

41

take over this farm. This farm that my dad worked with his bare hands and that his dad worked with his bare hands was going to be entrusted to you."

Taking advantage of the pause, Joseph responded, "Dad, I don't want to run the farm. I have been here for the last twenty years. There are other things I want to do." Joe shook the hot sauce violently into the skillet, and the fumes from the heated peppers quickly filled the room, causing both men's eyes to water.

"That is what college was for, Joseph. You got out of the house and off the farm for a while. Now it is time to come back and assume your responsibilities." Joe sounded more forceful than he intended.

Devastated at his father's remarks, Joseph shook his head and slumped over in his chair. "Dad, they are not my responsibilities; they're yours. It is not my farm; it is yours. I was raised on a farm, but I am not a farmer."

Joe removed the bologna from the skillet and placed two slices on a piece of white bread. He covered the open sandwich with another piece of bread and placed it in front of Joseph. Removing his hat, he retrieved his handkerchief and wiped his nose and eyes. He placed his hand on his son's shoulder. "You stop and see your aunt before you leave." Joseph wanted to reply but he sat still. He looked at the lunch he and his dad had shared for years and flinched when he heard the screen door slam shut.

Moments later, Joe looked up to see Joseph's car and the cloud of dust rapidly moving away from the farm. He picked up the wrench and went to work changing the attachments on the tractor. Again, the wrench slipped. Joe threw the wrench across the grassy expanse and watched it land some fifty feet from the tractor. He removed his hat and looked at the handkerchief inside. Then for the first time in many, many years, Joe wept.

Chapter 8

Matt and Sarah made their way through the aisles of the drugstore. Matt would pick up items he thought were needed and handed them to Sarah. She held a box of toothpaste, a toothbrush, deodorant, and for some reason, a lightbulb. Duke sat patiently in front of the drugstore and looked out over the town square. He would turn his head occasionally to see if Matt and Sarah had made their way to the cash register.

The store was not crowded, but there were several people milling about this afternoon in the various aisles. Each one spoke to Matt as he or she passed. "Well, hello, Preacher," said Ms. Ward as she moved past the toiletries. She stared hard at Sarah as she slowly walked by with her empty cart. Matt tipped his hat and smiled. Sarah stared hard back at Ms. Ward.

"Can we go now?" asked Sarah.

"Just a couple more things," replied Matt. "Don't you want to be prepared for your trip?" Sarah just shook her head and grunted.

As they were looking at the wonderful selection of candy bars—a section that Sarah was finally interested in—an older gentleman approached the two. Sarah watched the man walk steadily, but slowly, toward them, but Matt was too busy trying to decide between a Zero and a Zagnut to notice. Finally, the man reached them and stopped.

Sarah figured the man to be close to seventy years old. He had once been a big man, but a lifetime of labor had taken its toll on his body, and he now slumped forward and bent toward the ground. His hands were swollen around the knuckles, and his fingers were bent strangely toward his palms. He removed his felt hat and smiled at Sarah. Her lips creased in an upward angle at the sides in something that closely resembled a smile. With his arthritic hand, the man reached out and grabbed Matt's elbow.

"Paul," Matt surmised as he turned around. "How are you today?"

"Not well," replied Paul Gentry. "Millie is not doing well, Matt," he continued. "She has got a bad cough and her lungs are full of fluid. I have beat her back so much that she has bruises." Mr. Gentry's eyes became moist and he paused.

Gathering himself, he continued, "The doctor has sent me over here to pick up some medicine he prescribed. It doesn't look good, Matt. Do you think you could stop by? Millie would love to see you."

Sarah noticed the question seemed to make Matt uncomfortable. He looked around the store, then he took a deep breath and exhaled. He replied, "Sure, Paul. I will stop by this evening."

Mr. Gentry seemed pleased at Matt's response, but his eyes became moist once again. He said nothing, but nodded and put his hat back on his head. He smiled at Sarah and patted her on the arm before turning and making his way to the drug counter. For the first time in a very long time, Sarah felt compassion as she watched this man walk away.

"Shouldn't you go right now?" she asked Matt. He didn't respond. She continued, "I mean, it sounds real bad, don't you think? Shouldn't you go over there as soon as you can, just in case ... well ... you know." Matt still didn't respond.

"You sure are a tough one to figure, mister. Most preachers I have met are carrying their Bible, even when they are choosing to be in the wrong, but you—I haven't seen you with one yet. Also, you don't seem to be doing much God or Jesus talk for a preacher man. Most preachers I have come across would have told me lots about my eternal damnation by now, but you haven't said anything. Now, you don't want to go see this lady. Seems strange to me, that's all."

Matt looked at Sarah. He started to say something, but changed his mind. Taking a second to form his thoughts, he said, "I have been trying to get you to talk all day and you won't, but now you decide to spill your thoughts. Wonderful." Sarah started to speak back, but Matt held up his hand, signaling it was best for her to stop.

"Sarah," he said firmly as a father would address a child in a lesson, "life is a long, hard journey, and sometimes you simply don't know where you are on the map in relation to everybody else. You don't get it, and I don't expect you to, but I do care about Mr. and Mrs. Gentry, and I will go see her. For now, however, we are going to pay for these things and go see Naomi."

Sarah, putting her guard back up, responded curtly, "Don't flip your wig, man."

Chapter 9

Naomi sat atop the bicycle that had become her trademark mode of transportation. She had a car, and she did choose to drive it when the weather was bad, but on most days she could be found riding home from school on her light-yellow bicycle, complete with a wicker basket on the front and large white-walled tires.

She smiled as she turned the corner and headed back to her house as she thought about the wonderful day she had experienced. Her happiness grew as she turned into her drive and recognized the banged-up and dented car sitting in the driveway. Putting her feet down, she looked toward the house. There, sitting in the front porch swing and smiling back at her, was Joseph.

"Hey, Aunt Naomi," he called, jumping up from the swing and starting down the steps.

"Look at you," Naomi said as she grabbed his cheeks and kissed him. "What did I do to deserve such a wonderful surprise—especially in the middle of the week?" Joseph gathered her books from the wicker basket and carried them up the steps as Naomi opened the door.

"I came to talk to Dad," said Joseph, a serious look shadowing his face. Naomi, hearing the tone in his voice, put her arm around him and led him through the open door.

Joseph set Naomi's books on the coffee table as they entered her sitting room, then took a seat on her couch. Naomi sat on the chair across from the couch and leaned forward with her elbows on her knees and her closed hands next to her mouth. She looked at Joseph with compassionate eyes as she asked, "What happened, Joseph?" The young man sat back and laid his head against the back of the sofa and proceeded to give Naomi the account of the meeting with his father.

Naomi was torn as she heard the details of the discussion. She knew that Joseph was old enough to make his own decisions and to lead his own life, but she also knew that Joe had been working hard to have something to leave his son. Now it seemed as if his son did not want what Joe had to offer. It was not that Joseph was not appreciative; it was just that he did not want the life his father wanted for him.

She thought of her conversation with Peter earlier in the day. "I haven't told my father yet," Peter had said regarding his scholarship. Naomi thought it was strange that sons, so worried about disappointing their fathers, would simply stop communicating, and in the process, actually disappoint their fathers. It was an unfortunate circle of life in her experience.

Joseph blew an exasperated breath and slapped his knees. "Well," he said, "I have a long drive back, and I am pretty tired, so I better go."

"Joseph," Naomi said as they both stood. "Your father loves and supports you. He always has." She grabbed his arms and looked up at him. "What you are doing, it seems different to him, and it's not what he thought would happen. He will come around; you just have to give him time. In the meantime, you have to have patience with him."

Joseph nodded knowingly, but also showing his doubt. Then he put both his arms around Naomi and hugged her. "Where would I ever be without you?" Joseph asked.

Naomi grabbed his cheeks again, cherishing the question from her nephew. "We have learned a lot from each other."

They walked out the front door and onto the porch. Naomi stood at the top of the steps and watched Joseph walk back to his car. As they were outside, Matt's green pickup pulled up in front of the house. Matt honked the horn repeatedly while Duke jumped up into Sarah's lap and barked out the window.

Joseph and Naomi laughed at Duke's enthusiasm, while Sarah had a very different reaction. She covered her ears and kept telling Duke to, "be quiet!"

Matt leaned over, pulled Sarah's hand off of her ear, and whispered, "You should probably open the door."

Sarah reached over and grabbed the handle, opening the door and allowing Duke to launch himself from the seat of the truck and bound into the yard. He sprinted to Joseph, stopped in front of him, and quickly rolled onto his back. Joseph, laughing, knelt down and scratched his good friend's belly.

Matt exited the truck and passed in front of it as he made his way to Joseph and Duke. Smiling, he extended his hand. Joseph stood and grasped Matt's hand. With his free arm, Matt pulled Joseph in and hugged him tightly. "My boy," he said, "so glad to see you." He added a little extra pressure on the embrace and then let Joseph go. Their arms around each other, Joseph walked Matt to the porch. Duke was still lying on his back on the grass, waiting for Joseph to return.

Sarah slung her legs out of the truck and stood on the lawn, looking toward the porch. Her stomach felt empty again, and had it not been for the candy bar in the store earlier, she would have had no lunch. She was used to missing meals, however, so she took a deep breath and chose to ignore the hunger pangs once again. She slammed the truck door loud enough for the group on the lawn to hear. Pausing in their conversation, they looked toward Sarah, and Matt beckoned her up with an exaggerated waving motion.

She walked across the lawn toward the group. Duke, recognizing the opportunity to maintain some of his dignity, met her halfway and walked with her to the steps. Matt looked at Sarah and nodded at Joseph. "Sarah, this is Joe's boy, Joseph. He must have gotten lost on his way to work this morning."

Then shifting his gaze to Joseph, he continued, "Joseph, this young lady is Sarah. She is heading to Mexico and got stuck with us three geezers for breakfast this morning." Joseph and Sarah looked at each other, half smiled, and nodded.

"Well, I wish I could stay, but I have got to get back," Joseph said while taking a step toward Naomi. Naomi opened her arms and wrapped them around Joseph's neck one more time as he kissed her on the cheek.

"I love you, Aunt Naomi," he said as he turned away. "Matt, try to keep my dad out of trouble," Joseph said with a grin as he shook Matt's hand.

"Son, I am a preacher, not a miracle worker," Matt said as he slapped him on the shoulder.

As Joseph passed Sarah, he leaned in and whispered, "Good luck with this crew." Sarah laughed. Duke instinctively rolled on his back as Joseph approached him. Joseph gave him a good scratch on the belly and said, "See ya, Duke." Then he walked to his truck, entered the driver's door, and started the ignition. Matt and Naomi waved from the porch as he backed down the drive. He honked the horn a few times as he drove away.

"What is going on?" Matt asked Naomi as soon as the truck was out of sight.

"Oh, everything is okay," replied Naomi, "just a little disagreement between father and son. That's all." Then she looked at Sarah. "Did this man feed you today?"

"Well, we had candy bars," Sarah replied.

Naomi looked at Matt and shook her head. "*We*, huh?"

"Well, it has been a bit of busy day, and I couldn't let her eat alone," Matt said, nodding at Sarah for her help. Sarah did not oblige.

"Come on, get in here, and we will make some snacks to tide you over until dinner," Naomi said while opening the door and waving her hand for Sarah to come in.

Duke was the first one through the door, followed by Sarah. Matt hesitated though. "Naomi, I ran into Paul Gentry at the drugstore today. Do you mind if Sarah and Duke stay with you while I go see Millie?" Naomi looked at Matt. Just saying the names brought anguish to his eyes.

"Why don't you call Joe and ask him to go with you? After all, he could probably use some of your company after his argument with Joseph," she suggested.

"No, I should probably go alone. She is not doing well Paul said. But I will pick up that old stick-in-the-mud on my way back if you don't mind cooking for us," Matt suggested with raised eyebrows.

"You have been planning that out since this morning, Preacher," Naomi said with a laugh. Matt shrugged his shoulders and gave a look of exaggerated innocence as he made his way down the steps. "Matt, how did the day go with Sarah?" Naomi called after him.

"Well, I think she thinks I am a hip old guy." Sarah heard his reply through the screen door and laughed out loud.

Matt walked toward his truck, and Naomi opened the screen door and stepped inside. Sarah stood in front of the couch, and Duke sat beside her with his head cocked to one side. They both watched Naomi as the door shut behind her. Naomi noticed that Sarah looked much more tired than she appeared earlier at the diner and, standing in her living room; the young lady looked vulnerable and sad.

Naomi smiled at her and said, "You must have had a long day with Matt. Take a seat, and I will get you something to drink and a snack." Waving her hand at Duke, she said, "You, sir, come with me." Sarah nodded in understanding and sat softly on the sofa.

Sarah glanced around the living room in which she found herself sitting. Stacks of books stood on either side of the sofa and beside the two chairs facing her. The coffee table held an open Bible and three other open books with their pages facedown on the table to keep the place of the last page read.

There was a painting over the mantel on the fireplace. The colors were a beautiful mix of various shades in no particular pattern. For some reason, Sarah felt that it looked like a picture of a sunset. Probably because of the red, orange, blue, and slight purple hues that moved toward the top of the painting. The mantel held many pictures in many different types of frames. Sarah's curiosity got the best of her, and she rose from her seat and stepped toward them.

The first picture she saw was displayed in a small, brass, oval frame. The picture showed two young girls on the back of a pony. The girls looked so similar they could have been twins, but one was obviously two or three years older than the other. Sarah suspected the girls in the photo were close to eight and ten years old.

The next photo was a standard wedding photo with a smiling bride and groom. Looking closely, Sarah could tell that the man standing beside the groom was none other than Matt. He was much younger and had black wavy hair. Recognizing Matt in the picture made her examine the other people in the picture much closer.

She did not recognize the bride, but was certain the young lady standing next to the bride was Naomi. She laughed when she realized that the groom was Joe. He had a flattop haircut, and he was smiling from ear to ear. If Matt and Naomi had not been in the picture, she never would have recognized a smiling Joe.

Sarah surveyed the rest of the photos and was able to deduce that the bride in the photo was Naomi's sister. There were many pictures of the two at various ages. She could not help but think they were very close because they always seemed to be smiling or laughing at something.

As she worked her way to the right side of the mantel, she noticed that there seemed to be a large time gap between pictures. Suddenly, all the pictures contained the image of a baby. There was a picture of Joe in a military uniform holding the baby. Even though Joe was smiling, it was nowhere near the smile he showed in the wedding picture. His eyes looked sad, and his face looked drawn and tired. There were many pictures of Naomi holding the baby as well.

The next set of frames focused on the subject of a boy's growth into young man. The last picture was in a silver frame, and Sarah lifted it off the mantel. A young man, in his high school graduation robe and hat with a gold tassel, was flanked on the right by a smiling Joe and on the left by a smiling Naomi. Joe and the young man, Joseph, were smiling into the camera, but Naomi was looking at Joe.

Chapter 10

Matt sat in the driver's seat of his truck and gazed through the window at the house in front of him. The tan siding and brown trim looked a bit worn and were in need of a fresh coat of paint, but the yard was nicely manicured; likely a result of the Patterson boy next door. The flower beds in front of the porch, on either side of the front steps, were overgrown with weeds, and the roses had very few buds due to their lack of pruning. To Matt, this was a sure sign that Millie was not doing well.

He gripped the steering wheel and closed his eyes for a moment. He thought about saying a prayer, but decided against it. He was not in the mood and was not sure what good it would do anyway. For a moment, Matt was back on the beach and holding the young soldier in his arms. He could not go there, though—not right now.

Matt quickly opened his eyes and shook his head. He looked at his eyes in the rearview mirror and quickly looked away. He disliked the moments when his reflection showed him who he truly was. He took a deep breath in through his nose and blew it out hard through his mouth. He said to himself, "Okay, here we go," and opened the door.

As he made his way up to the porch, the front door opened. Through the screen door Matt could make out the shape of Paul. Matt stepped forward, and Paul opened the door with a squeak of the spring. "Thank you for coming, Matt. She will be so excited to see you."

Matt nodded at Paul and stepped through the open door. Paul let the door close behind him with the traditional slam of a screen door. "Wait just a moment while I tell her you're here. Okay, Matt?"

"Sure, Paul. Not a problem. Take your time, and if I need to come back later, then—"

"No, no. Please. Just one moment, and I will be right back." Again, Matt nodded and he took his hat in his hands.

The layout of most of the town's houses was the same. The Gentrys' home was laid out very similar to Naomi's house. Matt stood in their living room, looking at their fireplace. Above the fireplace was an eight-by-ten photo enclosed in an elaborate wooden frame with a folded American flag underneath.

The photo showed a young man standing with one foot on a sandbag and leaning against a jeep. His helmet was pulled back on his head revealing his hairline of jet-black hair. He held his rifle over one shoulder and flashed a bright smile at the person taking the picture. His eyes were full of life and seemed to convey happiness. Matt did not look at the picture long. He had seen it many times before.

Sitting on the mantel was a medium-sized box. Through a glass top, Matt could see small medals and ribbons. The awards surrounded a yellow piece of paper. Matt knew what it said, but he lowered his head to the glass to read it anyway. The paper was slightly faded beneath the glass of the box, but the prominent bold type of the Western Union logo still held an ominous meaning to Matt as he focused on it. Beneath the logo were pasted lines of printed tape. The tapes spelled out a message Matt knew by heart:

THE SECRETARY OF WAR ASKS ME TO EXPRESS HIS
DEEP REGRET THAT YOUR SON PRIVATE FIRST CLASS

WILLIAM PAUL GENTRY JR WAS KILLED IN ACTION
ON 6 JUNE IN FRANCE LETTER FOLLOWS ULIO THE
ADJUTANT GENERAL

Matt's eyes welled with tears, and he wanted nothing more than to rush from the room through the front door to the sanctuary of his truck. He knew that was not an option though. Not this time.

Almost as if waking from a slumber, Matt was startled by Paul's voice. "Matt. Are you okay, Matt?"

"Yes, Paul. I'm okay. I was just somewhere else for a moment," Matt said, slightly embarrassed.

"Reading that telegram seems to have that effect on me too," Paul said as he tried to offer a consoling expression, but came up a bit short. "Millie is ready to see you. She is very happy you are here." Paul raised his right arm and showed Matt back to the room where Millie lay in bed.

As Matt walked past him, Paul whispered, "She is very weak. Very weak." Matt nodded.

He stepped through the door and found Millie sitting up in her bed. Paul had helped her get into her housecoat and done what he could to fix her hair. Her face showed joy as Matt entered the room, but in doing so revealed the sharp angles of her cheeks and chin. She had lost a considerable amount of weight since the last time Matt had seen her. His best guess was that she weighed somewhere between eighty and ninety pounds. The fact that she was able to express any happiness surprised Matt.

Millie patted the side of the bed next to her. In a very weak voice, somehow still able to show excitement and hold on to her Southern accent, she said, "Please, Pastor, have a seat." Matt moved as directed.

"Now, Ms. Millie, you know to call me Matt."

"No," she answered. "I know I can call you Matt, but I prefer to call you Pastor." She fought off the urge to cough and arched her back a bit, giving Matt an expression of annoyance with the ordeal. Matt gently patted her on the leg.

Paul followed Matt into the room and sat in a rocking chair at the foot of the bed. Matt saw the pain on Paul's face as he looked at his dying wife. But, Paul seemed amused at the give-and-take between the two old pros.

"Pastor," Millie said in a near whisper, "not much longer now, and I will be with my Billy." A tear rolled down her cheek as she said the words.

Matt did not look, but he heard Paul's hard sniffles coming from his part of the room. Instead, Matt looked into Millie's eyes. Her eyes were a radiant blue, and they seemed so clear and expressive, even youthful. She reached out for Matt's hand, and he clasped her hand in both of his. He continued to meet her gaze and smile at her.

"Do you think he is waiting for me, Pastor? Do you think he is going to welcome me to heaven?"

Matt bit his lip and nodded. "Ms. Millie, I am sure of it." The words made Matt feel sick to his stomach, but he knew what she wanted to hear.

His thoughts kept trying to betray him and take him back to those moments with Millie's son on the beach at Normandy, but he mustered all of his strength to keep himself in the present. He could not go there. *Please God, not right now.*

Almost as if sensing his struggle, Millie placed her free hand on top of Matt's hand and strongly said, "Pastor Matthew Layne, it is not your fault that my son died. There is nothing you could have done. It was war, and war is terrible. You were with him and gave him peace, just like you are with me now."

The forcefulness of her voice caused her to fall into a brief fit of coughing. Paul fell to his knees beside the bed and put his hands on Millie's chest patting her with a perfect combination of firmness and gentleness. Millie moved her hands out of Matt's and wrapped them around the shoulders of her husband. The emotion in Paul's eyes revealed his silent grief.

Matt slowly patted Paul on the back and touched Millie's hand as he stood. Paul, still kneeling, continued to help Millie find relief from her congestion and raised his head. His eyes held tears, and sensing his wife's reprieve from coughing, he pulled a tissue from the bedside nightstand.

"Please forgive me, honey." He grasped Millie's hands. "I can't stand to see you in such distress."

Millie smiled at her husband and said, "Paul, my love, someday our family will be all together, and we will not remember any of this pain." Paul choked back his tears, returned his wife's reassuring gesture, and nodded his agreement.

Matt looked at the husband and wife and saw their true and abiding love for each other transcend the grief of the moment. They believed they would be together for eternity and that in this eternal life, they would be reunited with their son, who was taken much too soon.

His thoughts were broken by Paul's request: "Matt, could you pray for us?"

"I would love to," Matt responded, even though it was not what he wanted to do. Matt began, "Dear God—"

But Millie interrupted by saying, "Pastor, please kneel beside me, here. Let's hold hands." Matt placed his hat on the chair previously occupied by Paul, and stepped to the opposite side of the bed from Paul and slowly knelt. Millie grabbed his hand.

"Dear God," Matt began again, "the struggles of this life sometimes seem like too much to bear. Ms. Millie is sick, Lord, and while we do ask for her recovery, we also ask for her comfort. Be with Paul, oh God, as he calls upon You for strength and support. And God, if it is Your will, please let mother and child reunite with You in heaven when that time is upon them. In Your name, we pray—"

Millie interrupted, "Oh my heavenly Father, let Pastor Matt have faith in You again. He has been lost for too long now. Amen."

He glimpsed at Paul, who looked at Matt apologetically. Both men fixed their attention on Millie, who was very pleased with her addition to the prayer.

Matt stood and grabbed his hat from the chair. Paul stood also. "I will check on you soon, Ms. Millie," Matt said as he made his way toward the door.

"I won't be here," responded Millie matter of factly.

Stopping for a moment, Matt glanced back at Millie in the bed. Her eyes were shut, and her face held an expression of peacefulness. Matt shook his head and looked at Paul. Paul shrugged and curled his mouth on one side. Both men made their way to the front door in silence.

Matt stole a glance at the picture of Billy above the fireplace one more time as he walked through the living room. He opened the door and stepped onto the porch. Paul put his hand on Matt's shoulder, inviting Matt to turn around. He turned and extended his hand. Paul took Matt's hand in his while grasping Matt's elbow with the other. He tried to say something but was overcome with emotion and simply patted the back of Matt's hand instead.

"Call for me if you need me, Paul," Matt offered. Paul smiled, then quickly turned and went back through the door. After placing his hat on his head, he made his way to the truck. The door seemed to weigh five hundred pounds as he opened it, sat in his seat, and closed it behind him. He tried to breathe deeply, but he could not. Matt's palms were beginning to perspire, and his mind was returning him to the familiar sights and sounds of a battle that occurred nearly twenty years before.

Chapter 11

Sarah looked longingly at the long loaves of French bread she was slathering with butter. Her mouth was salivating so much she thought she would drool on the tray if she were not careful. Her struggle was not unnoticed by Naomi, who watched as she stirred the tomato sauce on the stovetop.

"Oh for goodness sake, Sarah, eat a piece of that bread," she encouraged with a laugh.

"Oh no … I mean, I'm not hungry," Sarah lied. But her stomach betrayed her and bellowed with a deep, long growl. They both laughed. Naomi grabbed a loaf of bread and tore a piece off, ripped it in two, then gave one piece to Sarah and took the other for herself.

Naomi took a bite of her half, then tossed the other piece to Duke who was following the food exchange most studiously. "See," she said, "it is the cook's prerogative to taste the food!" Sarah smiled.

Her smile faded to deep thoughts and broken memories, however. She imagined that this moment she was sharing with Naomi was what it must be like to learn to cook from your mother or grandmother. It made her heart feel cold to know that she had not experienced more of these moments. Naomi did not know her and did not care about her. For that matter, Sarah did not know Naomi and did not care about her. She was passing through. That was it, plain and simple. She was just passing through.

Naomi sensed that the mood had changed. Sarah now avoided looking her way, and her face was expressionless. Naomi thought for a moment, and then placed the lid on the saucepan as she turned down the flame under the pan.

"Sarah," she said, wiping her hands on her apron, "I think everything is done in here. While we are waiting on the fellows, let me show you to your room."

"My room?" questioned Sarah. "I didn't want to ... I mean, I don't need you to ..."

Naomi reached out and gently placed her hand on Sarah's shoulder. She moved close to Sarah and moved her head until Sarah's eyes locked on hers. "You are my guest, Sarah. You have a room and whatever else you need in this house. I am thankful you are here."

Tears came to Sarah's eyes, but she quickly looked down and stepped away from Naomi. "Thank you," she said. There was no attitude, there was no fight; there was only acceptance and genuine gratitude in her response.

~~~∞∞∞~~~

Matt had been able to regain his composure following his visit at the Gentry house, but his nerves were frazzled, and his head was spinning. He turned down Joe's drive, then rubbed his hands on his face quickly and wiped his nose with a handkerchief from his coat pocket.

The two men had known each other their whole lives. There was no way he could pull the wool over Joe's eyes. He would just have to be honest and let Joe know they would not be discussing this tonight. His truck pulled up to the porch, and he found Joe sitting on his steps, smoking his pipe.

Joe was putting away his handkerchief as he stood to greet his old friend. "How is it, Reverend?" Joe took one last, long pull from his pipe.

"I got a friend that has bad habits, but other than that, well …
okay," Matt joked.

Joe began the ritual of clearing, cleaning, and stowing his
pipe. "Well, you shouldn't talk about Ms. Naomi while she isn't
here, Matt, but I am sure her bad habits are better than my good
ones." Both men laughed.

Matt could see that Joe's face showed the stress and dismay of
a long and tenuous day. Joe could read the anguish that sat behind
Matt's eyes. They seemed to acknowledge that both were in a
difficult spot, and as they shook hands, they sealed a nonverbal
contract that tonight, each would let the other off easy.

"I'm hungry, Matt; how about you?"

"Starving," Matt replied. "What do you suppose Naomi is
making?" In unison they both said, "Spaghetti."

~~~

Sarah sat on the bed in the room Naomi had showed her. After
showing her where the powder room and the towels were, she told
her to take her time and make herself at home. She would call her
when the men arrived. Duke had followed them around like it
was some sort of parade, but when Naomi left, he stayed behind
and laid with his head on his paws on the carpet at Sarah's feet.

Her duffel bag was beside her on the bed, and she pulled the
string loose, allowing her to gain access to the contents. She pulled
out several of the new outfits from the church clothes closet. She
had nearly forgotten about her trip there that morning. It seemed
so long ago.

Sarah reached further into the bag and pulled out one of
her old shirts. She began to slowly unfold the shirt to reveal
a black-and-white photo in a silver frame. Using the shirt, she
gently wiped the glass of the frame and removed her fingerprints

from the silver sides. The silver was tarnished, but it still revealed fingerprints.

The picture portrayed the image of an American family in wartime. The young man was in an army dress uniform, and he stood nearly at attention as he looked forward with a large smile below a thin mustache. His hand rested on a beautiful young woman's shoulder as she sat in front of him. Her hair was long and dark, and she wore it neatly fashioned above her head. Her eyes were light and very bright in the photograph, almost illuminating the center of the picture.

On her lap she held a young girl, maybe two or three years old, in a dress with ruffled bloomers. The young girl had curly hair; she looked different than her mother, but bore the same beautiful eyes. At the bottom of the picture, just below the hem of the woman's dress, the top of her boots could be seen. The boots could not go unnoticed because they were embellished with beautiful, angel-wing embroidery.

Just then, Sarah heard a knock on the door and the voices of Matt and Joe as they greeted Naomi. Duke obviously heard the voices as well. He jumped to his feet, running. His actions made the rug bunch up under his feet until he touched the solid wood floor, then he was off.

"That dog is nuts," Sarah said to herself. She fixed the rug with her feet and folded the picture back into her shirt, then placed it back in the duffel bag.

Naomi knocked on the open door and announced, "Time to eat."

Matt and Joe were seated across from each other at the table, but they stood when Naomi and Sarah walked into the room. As the ladies took their seats, the men found theirs once again. Duke placed his head on Matt's leg and received the scratch behind his ear from his long-lost companion. Naomi and Joe both looked at Matt. Sarah looked at the other two, then followed their gaze to Matt.

Matt looked as if he were lost in a different world. He looked down at Duke's head and continued to scratch behind the dog's ear. Feeling the quiet, and that he was being watched, he looked up. The other three regarded him expectantly.

"Oh yes," he finally said. "God, bless this food. Amen."

Joe reached for a piece of bread and added, "Wow, Matt. You really dug deep for that one."

The four sat, eating in silence, until finally Naomi could stand it no longer. "Well, I had a good day today—actually, I had a great day," she exclaimed. "Peter is going to the university, and Joseph stopped by to see me. Not to mention, I met a new friend." She winked at Sarah. "And I am hosting a dinner party." Naomi paused, beaming triumphantly at each of them. "My day was glorious!"

Matt and Joe put down their utensils, glanced at each other, then at Sarah, then broke into applause. Naomi stood as if she had just received an ovation from the audience at Carnegie Hall. She curtsied and waved her hands in all directions, accepting the acknowledgment of her guests. Sarah sat bewildered.

As Naomi returned to her seat, Joe broke his silence by saying, "I was glad to see Joseph too. I am afraid he did not care too much to see me though," he continued. "Joseph does not want to take over the farm. He wants to stay in the city and make his life there." Matt took a bite of his spaghetti while watching Joe.

"Everything I have worked for. Everything I have done was to give that farm to Joseph. It is all I have, and now ... well, now he does not want what I have to give him."

Naomi placed her hand on his. "Joe, that is not all you have to give him."

Joe shook his head. "You know what I mean, Naomi."

"Yes, I do know," she replied. "Why do you think he drove all of this way to talk with you about something he could have written in a letter or said over a telephone call?" Joe looked at her with a quizzical expression.

"He loves you, Joe, and he looks up to you, and he wants you to be proud of him for who he is. It means everything for him. What you have to give, you old stubborn farmhand, is your blessing."

Matt took another bite of his spaghetti, watching Naomi.

"I think he is making a bad decision. How can I give my blessing on that?" Joe asked.

Sarah felt the anger growing inside her. She had seen this type of stubbornness play out before, and she knew how it ended … in pain. She only meant to talk in a normal tone, but it came out loud, and her eyes filled with tears: "Why do parents do that? Why do they torture their kids by ignoring them or telling them they are not good enough or that they are stupid?"

She put her head in her hands and began to cry. "I'm sorry," she said. "I have heard all of this before." Embarrassed, she rose from the table and hurriedly walked toward her room. Matt took another bite of his spaghetti.

Naomi, Matt, and Joe finished their meal without saying a word. As they were clearing the table, Naomi suggested, "All right, you two do the dishes. I will check on Sarah." She started to move toward the hallway, but Joe held out his hand.

"I'm the one who upset her. I will speak with her." Naomi and Matt looked at one another in apparent disbelief.

"Joe, the key word is *gentle*," Matt cautioned.

"Got it," said Joe as he made his way to Sarah's room.

He knocked on the door and slowly pushed it open. "Sarah," he said, "are you still hungry?"

"No," she replied almost in a whisper. "I'm sorry I ruined dinner," she said through tears.

"Young lady, it takes a lot more than that to ruin our dinners around here," Joe reassured her. "Look, Sarah, I love my son, and I am proud of him," Joe began. "I'm sure your parents feel the same way about you. Why, maybe if you picked up the phone and—"

"Look, mister," Sarah replied in a much stronger voice while drying her eyes, "my parents feel much different about me than you feel about your son. I know that, and I don't pretend any otherwise. So, don't you pretend either." Sarah was finding her rigidness again.

"Your talking reminded me of a conversation that happened a long time ago. That's all. They don't want me, and I don't want them; especially not now."

Joe nodded, then turned to leave the room. He stopped for a moment, placed his hand on the door frame, and turned his head halfway back to the room. "I am sorry you have been hurt so badly." There was just silence as he turned and made his way back to the kitchen.

"So, how did it go?" Naomi asked as Joe returned.

"I think she was reminded of a tough time. I have to say, I feel like a heel that it was me that reminded her of it," said Joe.

"Joe, she has been hanging out with us all day. She was bound to let off some steam sooner or later," Matt reassured his friend as he handed him a cup of coffee.

Naomi put her arm around Joe and rested her head on his shoulder for just a moment. "You need to talk to your son and work this out. You are both very good men."

Joe sipped his coffee. "I know. I suppose I forget sometimes that he is a man. He is a good one because of you."

"Well, Joe, I believe you just gave me a compliment," Naomi said as she slapped him on the shoulder. Joe smiled and steadied the coffee cup in his hand to prevent it from spilling.

Matt enjoyed seeing Naomi and Joe together. Life was complicated between them, but somehow, they were able to navigate through the waters to reveal a relationship that was real and binding. Both would claim to be friends with the other, but there was so much more that existed between them. She made him a better man, and he made her feel special. The connection was effortless between them and, although neither would admit it, they were in love.

Matt dared not say anything, even jokingly, about the two as it might break the chemistry for one reason or another. But he hoped one day they would be able to break the chains of the past and hold each other in the way in which they dreamed.

Joe startled Matt from his thoughts a bit as he slapped him on the back. "Preacher," he said, "it has been one heck of a day."

"That it has. Indeed it has ..." Matt trailed off.

"How was Ms. Millie, Matt?" Joe asked, somewhat reluctantly.

"She's dying, Joe. She will be gone soon, I'm afraid," Matt replied. Naomi and Joe shared a quick glance and closed their eyes for a moment.

"Does she need anything or want anything?" asked Naomi.

"No," Matt said, straightening himself from his resting position on the counter. "She is ready to go." He paused, shook his head slightly, "She thinks Billy is waiting for her on the other side."

He looked at the last swallow of coffee remaining in his cup and swirled it before tossing it in the sink. He rinsed the cup and set it in the basin. "It makes for a good fairy tale, I suppose," Matt said, positioning his hat on his head. Joe took the signal that it was time to go.

Sarah, who had been standing against the wall outside the kitchen door, heard the men begin to thank Naomi for dinner and say their good-byes. She quickly and quietly made her way back down the hall to her room and gently shut the door before lying down on the bed. She heard the voices fade and the front door close.

Footsteps made their way down the hall, and she heard her door open. She closed her eyes, pretending to sleep. She felt Naomi take her hand and push her hair back behind her ear. "Good night, Sarah," Naomi softly whispered into her ear.

Sarah heard the door close again, and she opened her eyes. She felt safe and comfortable. It was a feeling she had not experienced in a very long time. Her eyes became heavy, and she drifted off to sleep.

Chapter 12

The day had been a long one, and Matt was relieved to be in his bed. It is odd, he thought, how one can go through so many days that are seemingly identical, but then, out of nowhere, a day evolves bringing change and excitement that will likely alter the future days to come. After one of those days, the definition of "normal" changes, and the future can be sought with much anticipation or dreaded with great anxiety.

Matt was not sure where he stood on this day. It was much different than the last day he experienced that caused such change, and now, it was that previous day that occupied his thoughts. He threw himself on his bed and stared at his ceiling as he remembered the sights, sounds, smells, and … fear of that horrible day on the beach so long ago.

As he waited aboard a landing ship hundreds of yards from the beach, he could see the smoke billowing from the sites where flashes had occurred only moments before. The wind and the waves muffled the sounds coming from the raging battle, but unfortunately, the explosions and continuous gunfire could still be heard.

His body shook with fear and excitement. The adrenaline racing through his system caused his heart to beat rapidly and, at times, it felt like it would beat through his chest. He gripped the Bible in his hands and turned to the psalm he knew by heart, but needed to read at the moment. Slowly and steadily he began to read Psalm 23 aloud.

There was a shout from the front of the boat, and the vessel turned into the waves. Matt sat on the deck of the boat, knowing the next time he saw the beach he would be standing on it—if he was lucky enough to make it out of the boat. He stowed his Bible in his pocket, quickly checked the contents of his Communion set, closed his eyes tightly, and began to pray.

The memory of the landing was foggy, but at the same time, vivid in Matt's thoughts. Perhaps this was his mind's way of taming the violence and chaos of those brief minutes. He saw the memories in shadows and outlines and heard sounds in snippets, but he was unable, and unwilling, to replay the scene in its full detail.

The surf had carried the boat into the beach, and it had rammed another vessel upon landing. The men tried to open the door, but the collision allowed the hatch to only open halfway. The men had to run toward the remaining bulkhead and try to jump or climb over it to find their way to the battle on the beach. The action prevented the men from firing their weapons for protection and, as a result, only one in three attempts of exiting the boat was successful.

Matt stayed in the boat and attended to the wounded men as they fell back to the deck, covered in blood and screaming in pain. Gunfire rattled the steel of the boat's hull, but very few bullets found their way inside the vessel.

Having done what he could for the men in the boat, Matt knew he had to make his own exit. He was among the first chaplains to reach the battlefield, and he knew that he did not have the luxury of time. The sound of the bullets hitting the landing boat was not as frequent, so Matt believed he stood a very good chance of clearing the bulkhead safely. His problem was not knowing where to go once over the obstacle. He could possibly be in the wide open without cover when he made his exit. That was a chance he had to take.

He crossed himself, said a very quick prayer, and moved hard and fast toward the broken hatch. He reached out his two hands and grabbed the top of the bulkhead. He was fooled a bit by the angle at which the door was trapped, and his back foot caught the top of the door as he flung himself over.

On the other side of the boat, he hit the sand and water with the side of his body. The impact knocked the breath out of him, but he quickly came to his senses and looked for available cover. Twenty yards ahead of him was another landing boat, likely in further as a result of landing during a higher tide. He set his bearings on the boat and made a dash for its protection.

Gunfire erupted around him, but not as much as he had anticipated. Luckily for Matt, the Allied Forces had successfully encroached upon the German defenses and pushed them back off the coast. Only remnants of the German troops remained, and they were quickly being dealt with by the forces that had made their way up the dunes. Matt surveyed the beach from behind the boat and saw vast craters still smoldering from the explosions that had created them. There were men lying on the beach—some were moving and calling out for help; others showed no signs of life.

Some men were walking as if in a daze, not knowing what they were looking for or where they were headed. Many of these men were wounded, some very seriously. Medics ran feverishly from man to man, doing what they could to field dress the wounds and provide any relief from the pain they were able. About ten yards from Matt, a medic worked to bandage the leg (or what remained of the leg) of a man likely hit by shrapnel. Matt cleared his head from the fear and went to work alongside the medic.

As the day wore on, Matt and the medic moved from soldier to soldier. Sometimes the medic would have to stay with an individual soldier for a lengthy period of time, and Matt would move among the other soldiers in the area. If he came across a soldier who had died from his wounds, Matt closed their eyes and offered a prayer for him and collected one of his dog tags.

Even though he was not required to do so, he would write a letter to the family of each man he held a tag for. As he completed a prayer and placed his hand on the chest of a young marine, the medic called him and said he was moving on. Together they ran to the next soldier.

They ran hastily toward the next fallen soldier, but something caused Matt to pause, and he slowed his pace to a few steps behind his companion. The medic arrived at the soldier and rolled him from his facedown position in the sand. As the soldier was turned, he screamed in pain. An explosion had occurred so close to him that he was badly burned on the side of his face and neck, and his uniform was charred.

The medic's exam revealed multiple wounds from shrapnel on the young man's visible flesh, but many more grave wounds to his midsection and extremities. Bullets had pierced the young man in several locations, leaving a large wound in his stomach and nearly severing his right hand and lower left leg. There was nothing the medic could do other than administer a small dose of morphine to help with the pain.

An uneasy feeling came over Matt as he approached the young soldier, and he was brought to tears as he saw the young man's face. Billy Gentry looked up at Matt for a moment and then seemed to look past him and into the sky.

"I don't see them, Preacher," he said.

"You don't see who, Billy?" Matt asked, reaching for the soldier's good hand.

"The angels," he replied. "Not one."

Matt fumbled for his Bible and turned quickly to Psalm 27 and read, "Hear, O Lord, when I cry with my voice: have mercy also upon me, and answer me. When thou saidst, Seek ye my face; my heart said unto thee, Thy face, Lord, will I seek."

Billy started to groan from the pain and the morphine taking effect in his body. He reached for the Bible with his bloody hand, and deep-red blood fell across the thin pages of the badly worn Bible.

Matt gently grasped the wrist of the young man's arm and held it strongly as he continued, "Hide not thy face far from me; put not thy servant away in anger: thou hast been my help; leave me not, neither forsake me, O God of my salvation."

"Pastor Matt," Billy said as he began to cry, "please tell my folks I love them."

"I will, Billy. I promise, I will," Matt responded, putting his hand on Billy's forehead and pushing his hair back out of his eyes. The eyes that looked up at him were frightened and losing life. Matt was not sure what to say or to do to console the young man.

Unfortunately, he had been in this same situation with many other soldiers, but he had watched Billy grow up from a boy to a man. He saw him pitch the no-hitter game that got them into the state finals, and he rode on the bus with the team when they lost the final game. He was there when Billy was baptized and the church officially became his family.

He knew this young man better than he could have known another man on the battlefield. Matt had helped raise Billy, and he was the perfect symbol of the small town they were from. He embodied the town's best attributes and the strongest hopes. This young man, this good boy, was dying.

"Billy, would you like to pray with me?" Billy nodded, still looking past Matt and to the sky—waiting, hoping to see something. Matt began with the Lord's Prayer. He kept his eyes on Billy as he prayed. Billy's gaze did not waiver, and his lips moved slightly in the rhythm of the prayer.

"Dear God," Matt prayed silently and concurrently with his outward prayer, "let Billy see You. Reveal Your awesome presence to this young man who has given everything in this life. Show Yourself, God! Please!"

Matt reached into his satchel and removed his Communion set. He removed a white tube with brass ends and unscrewed one of the ends. Tilting the tube, he was able to reveal and remove a Communion wafer from the container. He secured the top back on the tube and replaced the tube in the box. There was a small canteen in the box. It was not an original piece to the set, but it had replaced a wine container that Matt had fumbled on a previous battlefield that seemed like a lifetime ago. He looked at Billy, who still gazed toward the heavens.

"Billy, on the day before He died, Christ took the bread and broke it," Matt recited as he broke the wafer in two. "He gave the bread to His disciples and said, 'Take. Eat. This is My body that has been broken for you. Do this in remembrance of Me.'"

Matt placed the wafer in Billy's mouth. Then holding the canteen, he quickly removed the top and said, "This is Christ's blood, which has been shed for you," and he lowered the open canteen to Billy's lip. He poured so the wine gently touched the dry lips of the hurting young man. Billy chewed gently and swallowed, never averting his gaze into the sky.

Suddenly, Billy locked eyes with Matt and lunged toward him. Reaching out for Matt, he cried, "I don't see them! I don't see them! They are supposed to come for me! I don't see them! Please God, I don't want to die! Please, Matt, help me!" He struggled to pull himself up or pull Matt closer to him, but he was not strong enough to do either.

"Please help me!" Billy exclaimed hysterically. "I don't see them!" Then his eyes widened, and he became still. His body began to shake violently, then his breathing stopped. He lay on the wet sand, still looking to the heavens. Matt reached down and closed the boy's eyes gently, then he began to cry uncontrollably.

Not knowing how long he sat with Billy's body, he finally returned to the moment. He looked around the beach and could no longer see the medic he had teamed with earlier. The clouds seemed to have rolled in off the ocean, and a wall of humidity brought heaviness to the air.

Billy lay on the ground in front of Matt, lifeless. Matt placed his hand on the chest of the fallen soldier and sighed. Just like he had done so many times before, he removed one tag from Billy's chain, leaving the other to identify the lost soldier. Matt attached the tag to the ring he carried that held the other tags he had saved. He rose to his feet and pushed the caked sand off his worn clothes.

Matt noticed he had left his Bible on Billy's chest as he looked at the body before him. The ring of dog tags made a ringing sound as if it were a wind chime. Billy's face merged into the collage of the other faces that had been put to rest by the war and represented by the tags in Matt's hand.

The ravages of war and the loss of life that Matt had experienced over the past years of the war took hold deep in his soul. Just as Billy had become unable to see God's face and love around them, this man of faith and of utter confidence in his belief, for the first time began to doubt.

Anger flowed through his thoughts, and he turned and walked away, leaving the Bible and Billy. He had arrived on the beach, running frantically and trying to make his way to all of the soldiers he was able to, while preserving his own life. Now he moved slowly and cared very little if he were to fall into the crosshairs of a hidden sniper. ...

Matt slowly returned from his memories. He was aware that he had perspired through his pajamas and was crying uncontrollably. This was not an attack of anxiety or of fear; it was overwhelming sadness. The God he had so desperately believed in and sought to share with all who believed hope was unattainable; the God he firmly believed was the ultimate power of love; the God who cared enough for His creation to incarnate Himself as a human and be beaten and die for our sins—that God, that omnipotent God, was not on the beach the day Matt so desperately needed Him to be. In fact, he had convinced himself God was not with them in the war at all.

Matt had left his Bible with Billy and had not opened one another day since. He thought about Sarah's question to him earlier in the day about not carrying a Bible and how that seemed peculiar for a minister. It seemed strange that the question came on the day that Billy's mother needed to see Matt.

Matt, however shaken in his faith, was unable to abandon his belief in God. God was certainly real, but Matt no longer trusted Him. It was okay if others did, but Matt knew better. He returned from the war and remained a minister in the small town he had always known. The war had changed Matt forever, and his dreams and aspirations of saving those in the world who did not know God were dimmed in his heart.

Upon his return, the Baron had already begun buying up the real estate of the town and managing its politics. The church fell under those things, places, and people that were acquired, and Matt found it easy to fall into a role of a preacher who spoke about God without depth and who offered messages with benefit to Barrister Enterprises.

Millie had called him out on this ruse today though. For seventeen years, Matt thought he had been doing a good job of providing the town with a preacher, without actually committing himself to the faith required for the job. He baptized, he married, he performed burials, and he preached every Sunday. He still gave people hope, even though he did not believe the hope he offered was always available. Millie knew he was a fraud, and she wanted him to know she knew.

Her recognition of his secret was also magnified by his day with Sarah. This young lady, this poor girl, needed more than false hope. She needed help. There was something more to her story, and he needed to know what it was. His time with her revived feelings of a time long past where he wanted to really help those who needed to know love.

Sarah was not someone from the town who simply went through the motions with Matt; she was someone who was truly lost in her life. Meaningless sermons and simple blessings would provide her with nothing. She needed to know that she was not alone and that the world was not against her. She needed to know the God whom Matt thought he knew before that day on the beach with Billy. Matt knew he could not lead her to that God unless he, himself, was willing to search for Him again.

Matt stood from his bed and removed his soaked pajamas. Duke studied Matt as he moved to the sink and splashed water over his face. Matt looked into the mirror and examined the face of the man staring back at him. He had changed considerably from the person he was during the war. There were wrinkles and hair that was mostly gray and thinning.

But looking into his eyes, he still could see a small glint of the youthful excitement and zeal for a God he had mostly abandoned. He shook his head and returned to his bed, patting Duke's head along the way. With the covers pulled up to his chest, he looked at the ceiling and breathed deeply, hoping that he would soon fall asleep.

Chapter 13

The rumbling in her stomach woke Sarah, and when she opened her eyes, the wave of nausea overcame her. She leapt from her bed and barely made it down the hall to the bathroom before she became sick. Then she knelt on the floor with her hands draped across the seat of the toilet, seeking relief from the pains in her belly.

Sarah removed a tissue from the box on the sink and wiped her eyes and blew her nose. She fell back from her knees onto her bottom and leaned against the cold porcelain of the bathtub. The nausea remained, but she felt like she would be able to ward off another episode of sickness. She placed her hands on the side of the cream-colored tub and pushed herself up. As she steadied herself for a moment, she tried to judge the uneasy feeling in her stomach.

Green and tan washcloths sat on a shelf beside the sink. Sarah removed one of the cloths and ran cold water over the fabric. With both hands, she wrung the cloth out into the sink and then placed the cool cloth on her face, pulling it down the sides of her cheeks. After wiping her mouth, Sarah folded the washcloth and placed it on the back of her neck and gently dabbed the moist cloth against her skin. The coolness of the water made her feel a bit better and removed some of the dizziness the wave of nausea had brought on. She only hoped she had not woken Naomi.

As Sarah exited the bathroom, she noticed a light on in the kitchen. Despite having been so sick and still battling the nausea, she could not help but notice the pleasant smell of something cooking. Unbelievably, she was hungry. She looked at a clock on the hallway wall that read four thirty. It seemed very early to be awake, but Sarah decided to see what Naomi was doing. Plus, whatever it was that she smelled was pulling her toward the kitchen.

She turned the corner and entered the room. Naomi was sitting at the small, two-person table, in the corner of the kitchen. She greeted Sarah with a warm smile and pushed out the other chair at the table with her foot. In front of the chair on the table was a plate of buttered toast with sugar and cinnamon sprinkled on it and a cup of hot tea. Naomi sipped on a cup of tea as well.

Sarah made her way to the table and sat in the offered chair. "Thank you," she said, looking at the food in front of her. "I'm sorry I woke you so early."

Naomi shrugged her shoulders and ran her hand through Sarah's long hair, still damp from the washcloth. "It's okay, hon," Naomi reassured her. "You know, my sister battled morning sickness for five months with Joseph."

Stunned, Sarah turned toward Naomi and instinctively began to deny the implication. She thought better of the idea, however, and quickly averted her eyes and looked at the toast in front of her.

"How far along are you?" asked Naomi. Sarah breathed in deeply through her nose, causing her shoulders to rise, and then out through her mouth as her shoulders fell.

"Around two months," she responded, trying to fight the tears.

~~∞∞~~

Joe had not slept a wink after Matt dropped him off last night. The two men, both deep in thought, had barely shared a word on the ride back from Naomi's. Joe recalled the discussion as he laid in the dark. The car had slowed to a stop on the gravel drive in front of Joe's house. In unison, both men reached for the car handles, opened their doors, and pulled themselves out of the car.

Each man turned and rested his forearms on the hood of Matt's truck, its lights illuminating the crops in front of the house. Different insects began to dance in the beams of the headlights, and Duke watched the scene unfold from the center of the front seat.

"Quite a day, eh, Matt?" Joe finally said.

"Yep, quite a day," responded Matt. "What are you and Joseph going to do?" Matt figured Joe was ready to talk about it now.

"Matt, the boy lost his mom before he even knew her. I never had much to give him except hard work and advice," Joe responded. Stretching his arms out over the hood and looking down at the ground, then out over the farm, Joe continued, "I thought he would want to take over the farm ... I thought he loved the farm."

Matt watched his old friend and offered what solace he could. "Joe, you raised him to be his own man. You showed him the difference between right and wrong and what it means to earn respect. He has earned yours."

Joe smiled. "There you go again, trying to act like a preacher." He paused, "This is it, Matt," nodding toward the field. "This is the last crop. I may be able to pay off the bank when it is said and done, but likely not. I was keeping it going for Joseph, but I suppose this is all a blessing. It would have put a lot of pressure on him anyway."

Matt looked out over the field illuminated by the yellow light of the truck's beams. "It was a great run, Joe."

Joe pushed himself away from the truck. "Yes it was. But now it's time to move on."

Standing upright, Matt gave a tap to the hood of his truck. "I suppose it is."

Joe made his way toward the house, and Matt moved to the open driver's side door. "I don't think I will be around tomorrow," Joe said, pausing for a moment. "If you don't mind, will you let Naomi know so she doesn't worry?"

"Will do," responded Matt. Than he added, "Tell Joseph I said hello."

Since then, Joe had spent the night wondering what he would say to Joseph and how it would be received by his son. He was probably tougher with his son than most fathers had been on their children, but he had also learned to be soft and to show him love, largely because Naomi had helped teach him. Losing his mother was tough for Joseph, but the two had persevered through the loss together … again, with a large thanks to Naomi.

Perhaps just as prominent in Joe's mind was his relationship with Naomi and what she meant to him. It was so complicated though, or at least it seemed complicated. She was his wife's sister, and he had loved his wife. He felt he had abandoned his wife during the war and made her go through the rigors of carrying a child and experiencing a difficult birth alone.

He had not been there to tell her how strong she was or how much he loved her, as she lay dying in her hospital bed. His last words to her were at her grave as he held his newborn boy: "I will never love anyone else the way I love you."

~~∽∞∽~~

"The key," Naomi told Sarah as she stood, "is to keep something in your belly. If you eat too much or too little, it can make you feel all out of whack."

Naomi went to the stove and poured more of the hot water from the kettle into her cup and removed another teabag from a glass jar on the counter.

Sarah took a sip of her tea. "Have you ever been pregnant?" she asked Naomi. Without thinking, Naomi replied, "No. I have never been married." Quickly she realized what she had said and her face became flushed. "I'm sorry, dear, I did not mean anything. I just was being thoughtless."

Sarah was stung by the comment but refused to show it. As a defense she offered, "I am not going to have to worry about it for long anyway."

"Oh," said Naomi, "you plan on putting the baby up for adoption?"

"No," said Sarah, her eyes turning vacant and void of emotion. "In Mexico, they can stop you from being pregnant. That's why I am going there."

Naomi pulled the string on her teabag up and released it back down, allowing the tea in the bag to seep into the hot water. "I see," she said with sadness in her voice. "Are you sure that is what you want, Sarah?"

Sarah continued to look away from Naomi and nodded in the affirmative.

Naomi took a drink of her tea and allowed the warm cup to soothe her hands. She had only known this young girl for less than twenty-four hours, but she already cared for her a great deal. The burdens laid on the shoulders of this child must have been so difficult to bear, and now she sat in Naomi's kitchen, ill from the effects of a pregnancy for which she was not prepared.

She carried her tea with her as she prepared to go back to her room. Moving toward the hallway, Naomi reached out and touched the shoulder of the girl. "I'm sorry, Sarah," she said. "Finish up your toast and get dressed for the day," she continued, trying to sound more chipper. "We will get some real breakfast in a bit and see what the fellas are planning today."

Naomi stopped in the hallway and looked down at her cup of tea. "Sarah, I am glad you are in my house, and I am happy I met you." Naomi then continued to her room. Sarah, expecting to have been thrown out of the house, sat at the kitchen table in disbelief and wonder at Naomi's words.

~~~

At six thirty on Friday morning, Matt and Duke pulled up in front of Naomi's house. Sarah and Naomi were sitting on the porch waiting for Matt and made their way down the steps toward his truck. Naomi carried a bag holding some papers and other sundries for the school day, while Sarah carried her completely packed duffel bag.

Matt made his way out of the truck and took the duffel bag from Sarah. Hoisting it into the bed of the truck, he asked, "Going somewhere?"

"Yes," she replied, "Mexico." She stole a look at Naomi, who smiled at her empathetically.

"Oh yeah," Matt quipped, "I keep forgetting." Almost instinctively, Duke realized there were too many people for the cab, and he would be the lucky one to ride in the back. Matt lowered the tailgate, and his partner bounded in and lay down, putting his head on Sarah's bag. Matt returned to the driver's seat, Naomi sat in the center holding her bag, and Sarah looked out the passenger-side window.

As Matt pulled away from the curb, Naomi asked, "Is Joe meeting us there?"

Chapter 14

Joe threw his lunch pail, containing a bologna sandwich and apple, and his thermos of black coffee into his old Buick and started the engine. He bit into a three-day-old biscuit and sipped from a mug of coffee, thinking how much he missed the Blossom Dairy Diner this morning.

He looked through the front windshield of the car and could see the sun rising on the other side of his fields. The orange and red hues covered the deep green of the crops, and the plants glistened as the rays bounced off the morning dew. He loved this place. To him, it was what heaven must look like. He was sad that it would slowly fade away, but he was resolute in his decision to support his son. He put the car in drive and moved forward into the light of the rising sun.

It had been over a year since Joe had made the trip to Austin, and he stretched his arms against the steering wheel and moved his head in a circular motion to stretch his neck. He was only halfway there and felt as if he had been in the car for days. The lack of scenery and the lack of sleep combined to make his eyes heavy and his mind foggy.

In order to stay alert, he refilled his coffee cup regularly. His system of holding the cup and opening, pouring from, and securing the thermos was frequently performed. He was very fortunate there was little traffic and no turns on the long, flat road to Austin.

He had just poured his last drop of coffee, secured the lid, and tossed the empty thermos to the floor when he saw the tall buildings of the Texas capital coming into view. The sun was not yet in the middle of the sky above the city, but it cast shadows of the city in the direction of Joe's car.

The tall buildings were quite a change in the landscape from the farmlands and plains visible on the three-hour drive. The sight of the city emerging out of the landscape never ceased to amaze Joe. It was like some sort of magician's trick or optical illusion. Nonetheless, he was here, and his heart beat with excitement to talk with his son.

He navigated his car through the city streets, looking for Rio Grande Street. He knew Joseph's work address was on that street, and it was close to the Austin High School. Finally he came to a light and noticed the cross street was Rio Grande. Joe made the quick decision to turn right in hopes that he would see the school or the community center where his son worked.

Joe drove slowly as he examined the signs on the doors of the businesses lining the street on either side. After coming to a stop at a red light, he contemplated whether he had made the wrong decision and needed to turn in the other direction. He looked in his rearview mirror and saw nothing that would make the decision any easier. He must have turned the wrong way, he thought.

But just then, up ahead in the next block he saw a group of boys, maybe twelve years old or so, run across the street and enter a building on the right side. "That has got to be it," Joe said as the light changed and he pressed on the gas.

He pulled through the light and swung the big Buick into an opening on the right side of the street. He watched the door of the building about fifty feet in front and to the right of him for a few minutes, looking for other identifying activity. The door opened and a group of three boys came bounding out the door and down the front stairs, tossing a ball back and forth to each other as they talked and walked down the street. He could hear them laughing as they passed his car.

Firmly convinced he had found the right location, Joe grabbed his lunch pail and swung his legs out the driver-side door. He knocked on the hood of his car for luck as he walked in front of it and hopped onto the sidewalk. He felt good and was looking forward to seeing Joseph.

The front of the building was rather unspectacular. A storm door made of steel rods and a guarded pane of glass sat closed while a large wooden door was swung open on the inside. There was a small placard to the right of the door that read, "Austin Home for Boys." Someone had taken a sharp object and carved the words "and Girls" in the bottom of the sign. The brick building looked old, but in good repair. He pondered for a moment whether he should knock or walk right on in. He opted for the latter.

The screen door opened with a bit of a squeak and as it closed behind him, a bell rang. With the ringing of the bell, some of Joe's confidence left him. He thought about doing an about-face and hurrying out the door he had just come in. But a friendly face peeked around the corner from a room down the hallway.

"Well, hello there!" a young lady, maybe nineteen or twenty years old greeted Joe. She came walking up the hall. "I knew something was different when I didn't hear loud voices and lots of footsteps running down the hall."

She was an attractive girl with long brown hair, big brown eyes, and a crooked smile. "So, how can I help you?" she asked.

"Well, I was looking for Joseph … does he work here?" asked Joe, somewhat embarrassed he was not sure whether or not this was his son's place of work.

"Jo-*seph*," the girl said with a laugh. "Our director goes by 'Joe.' Maybe he is who you are looking for." She motioned for Joe to follow her down the hallway.

As they began walking, she continued to laugh. "'Joseph' sounds so formal. I think we should start calling Joe that even if he is not who you are looking for." Glancing back, she placed her hand to the side of her mouth and confided to Joe, "He is not really the formal type. I think he grew up on a farm in West Texas somewhere." Joe knew he was in the right place.

The girl came to a stop in front of the last door in the hallway. The door was slightly cracked, and she knocked on it before pushing it open wide enough to stick her head in. "Excuse me, Jo-*seph*; you have a visitor."

Joseph said something, and the girl laughed and pushed the door open the rest of the way. Joe stood in the door opening and looked at his son behind a stack of papers piled on a desk.

"Dad!" Joseph exclaimed. "What are you … I mean … why are you … please come in." Then noticing the young lady was still standing there with her mouth wide open, Joseph introduced them: "Jenny, this is my dad. Dad, this is Jenny."

Joe held out his hand, and she took it enthusiastically. Jenny looked at Joe, than looked at Joseph, then back at Joe. "Yep, I see it." Then she smiled at Joe on the way out. "Looks like he's got some good genes." Joe and Joseph laughed as she walked out of the office.

Joseph started to say something, but Joe held up his hand, indicating for him to stop. Joe held his lunch pail in his hand and gave it a lift to show it to Joseph. "I was wondering if you wouldn't mind having lunch with me?"

Smiling, Joseph reached down behind his desk and grabbed his own lunch pail. "Sounds good to me." He motioned to the door and said, "Follow me."

Joseph walked out first and led them to the back door marked "Fire Escape" at the very end of the hallway. He opened the door to the stairs leading into the building's courtyard.

"There are some picnic tables down here," Joseph said as he indicated the shady corner of the yard.

Joe came out onto the steps and looked around the yard. There were maybe fifteen or so girls and boys playing various games in the courtyard. Some of them were jumping rope and saying rhymes as the person in the center moved through the ropes. Joe got a smile on his face and followed his son down the steps.

They arrived at the picnic tables and sat on opposite sides, facing each other. "Sure is a great place for them to play," said Joe.

"And a safe place for them to play," added Joseph.

Both men opened their boxes and pulled out their single sandwiches for lunch. They gave sly grins to each other, knowing exactly what treasure the other one held. "Bologna sandwiches," they both said at the same time.

They laughed as they unwrapped the traditional family lunch. Joe took a bite and looked at his son. Joseph was watching the kids play and had a contented look on his face. The look made Joe proud. He knew his son was where he wanted to be, and from what he had seen in the first ten minutes, needed to be.

"You have made a nice place here, Mr. Director," Joe complimented while making it clear he was a little shocked he did not know the whole story behind Joseph's position.

"Yeah, Dad, about that … I would have told you, it just … well, the timing was never … you know," Joseph tried to explain.

"I get it, son. Believe me, I get it," Joe said, putting Joseph at ease.

The two did not say much, but they enjoyed the sights and the sounds of the children playing in the yard for a while after they ate.

Finally, Joe broke the silence. "Son, I was wrong yesterday. I didn't treat you like the man you have become, and I apologize for that."

Joseph looked at his father. He had admired this man his whole life and wanted nothing more than to make him proud. His father had just said two things that caused him to take notice. First, he had apologized, which was new to Joseph, and second, he called him a man.

"Thanks, Dad," Joseph said, "but I wasn't entirely fair to you either. I sprang something on you without giving you much notice."

"Yes. Yes, you did, but I suppose you have tried to tell me in your own way for a while now," Joe said, shifting in his seat some and mustering up the courage to make the speech he had driven all this way to make.

For comfort and courage, Joe removed the handkerchief from his pocket that held his cherry pipe. Joseph watched his father perform the ritual of carefully unwrapping the pipe and filling it with the sweet-smelling cherry tobacco. Joe did not light the pipe, but held it in his mouth for a few moments, allowing his senses to be enveloped by the feel, smell, and taste of the pipe and its contents.

In a gruff voice Joe began, "Joseph, your mother, God rest her soul, was a wonderful woman." Joe looked up into the blue sky, remembering her warm smile and beautiful eyes. He was sure she was delighted in seeing him squirm, but was proud of him for setting their son free.

"I was a hard young man, but that woman made me melt." They both laughed. "I never thought that the hard shell I had built from my years of working on the farm in the dirt during the hottest days and soggiest downpours would be penetrated by something as soft and delicate as your mother."

Joe looked down at the table, then met his son's eyes. "But she did, and I loved her like God intended for a man to love a woman."

Pausing a moment to clear his throat and keep his faculties together, he continued, "The day she died, I lost some of that softness because my heart became hard again. Save for one thing, this baby who was part of her and part of me, now needed me to care for him." He removed the pipe from his mouth and pointed the stem at his son. "You were the greatest gift your mother ever could have given me because you are the best of both of us."

The statement unsettled Joe for a moment, and he paused to let himself regain his composure. He reached into his pocket and pulled out the handkerchief that did not hold his pipe, and he wiped his eyes and brow with it. Joseph sat spellbound by his father's speech. Tears slowly rolled from the corner of his eyes, but he seemed unconscious of this. Joe did not acknowledge the emotions either.

"I never have had much to give you, son," Joe began in a more even voice. "I suspect the eighty acres and the farm was my idea of the legacy I had to offer you." Joe shook his head slowly. "I suppose that is what made it so hard to hear that you didn't want it."

Joseph began to speak, but Joe continued before he had the chance. "But then, we had dinner last night with a young girl who is lost and confused, and she made me realize that I had something to give you that she hadn't been given."

Joe straightened himself and held his pipe in his hands. He focused on the pipe for a moment, then he looked Joseph in the eye and said, "Joe, you are every bit the man I hoped and raised you to be. You do what you feel called to do, because it is your decision. I will stand by you, no matter what. That is my blessing, Joseph, that you will succeed in accomplishing whatever your heart wants you to accomplish."

Joseph was overcome by emotion and stood, turning away from the children in the yard and turning his back to his father. Joe watched his son's shoulders move up and down for a moment without knowing what to say. He took his pipe, without removing the unused tobacco, and folded it back up in the handkerchief. He placed both hands on his knees and pushed himself into the standing position. Slowly he walked to his son and placed one hand on his shoulder.

"I love you, Dad," Joseph said without looking at his father.

"I know, son, and I love you too," his father replied. Both men looked around the yard and noticed they were being watched. They turned and stood shoulder to shoulder, then slapped one another hard on the backs.

Joe examined his son for a moment. "You know. I still can't believe that all of my farming lessons didn't rub off on you one bit."

Joseph shrugged and replied, "Well, I suppose it just wasn't in my genes." Joe laughed and kicked at the loose gravel. "Dad," Joseph said, "before you go, I would like to show you something."

Joseph led Joe back to the fire escape, and they climbed up to the door leading to Joseph's office. To Joe's surprise, they passed the door and kept ascending the staircase. They passed each door giving entry to the building until finally reaching the last flight of stairs led to the roof.

Joseph looked back at his father and raised his eyebrows a couple of times and flashed his teeth in a big smile. Joe was not sure what to think of this peculiar behavior or this trip to the roof of his son's office building.

Joseph climbed the short ladder leading from the small landing to the top of the building. Once over the short wall, he looked back down and motioned for his father to follow. Joe shrugged and threw his hands up into the air. He stepped to the ladder and ascended the ten rungs to the top. Standing on the ladder and looking over the wall, he stopped in awe.

There were three rows of planter boxes about four feet wide and fifteen feet long, each arranged on the roof of the building. They were shallow, but the soil was certainly fertile as evidenced by the tomatoes, squash, and zucchini Joe saw right off the bat.

Joe climbed over the wall and walked toward the rooftop garden. There was a teenage boy harvesting small cherry tomatoes from the vine, and he offered Joe one of the tomatoes as a sample. The older man held the tomato between two of his fingers and looked at it, then popped the entire thing in his mouth. It was juicy and full of flavor. He looked at his son, who was standing back with a proud look on his face.

Examining the containers around the roof, Joe was most enamored with the irrigation system that had been developed. A large barrel collected rain at the end of each row. Hoses were attached to the barrel and fed below the soil in the containers. Joe grabbed a handful of soil beside the barrel and one at the end of the container. Both were moist.

Children who would never have known what it is like to grow their own food, now had the opportunity because of the rooftop garden. A scarecrow dressed like a football player in broad shoulder pads and a helmet wore the number seven and watched over the precious crops. Each row contained something different and in a different stage of growth. The last eight feet of the last container was double in its depth and held corn stalks nearly three feet high.

Joe made his way over to his son, and both stood and surveyed the rooftop farm. "It's beautiful, son," he told Joseph.

"Maybe I was wrong, Dad," Joseph said beaming. "It is in the genes."

Chapter 15

"Well, I can't believe he didn't tell anyone and just up and went," Naomi remarked, clearly irritated by Joe's decision to go to Austin.

"Sure he told somebody, Naomi." Matt added to her irritation by saying, "He told *me*." He glanced over at Sarah and winked. Naomi waved her hand and stuck out her tongue at the preacher.

The Blossom Dairy was pretty quiet, especially for a Friday morning. With the exception of two other tables seated with diners, Matt, Sarah, and Naomi had the place to themselves. Duke didn't seem to mind as he stayed out from under the table and beside Matt. Matt slipped him a piece of bacon every few minutes to keep him from wandering.

Matt's head hurt, and his nerves were raw. It seemed that since he had the episode the night before, he had been trying to recover—or more accurately, to battle any further escalations. His memories had taken him to a place last night that he tried to refrain from going. His head echoed with the sounds, sights, and smells of a time long past that he had done his very best to bury.

He had a pain in his left shoulder, right below his neck. It was a mix between a crampy pain and the pins-and-needles one would feel if a foot was asleep. Occasionally the pain would radiate down his back, his chest, his arm, or up his neck, causing him to take a deep breath and pause.

It was possible that these could be the symptoms of a heart attack or stroke, and that did nothing but exacerbate the experience. Yes, at times he welcomed the finality of death, but mostly he was scared of dying. This was certainly not something a preacher would publicize. He was lost in his thoughts when Duke nudged his hand, ready for another piece of bacon.

Sarah watched Naomi cautiously. She was somewhat relieved that Naomi had been caught off guard by Joe's trip to see Joseph. She just knew that it would not take long for Naomi to share her secret with Matt, and then the lectures would start. Worse, he might just wash his hands of her and want nothing to do with her.

She thought it strange that she found herself preferring the lecture to the abandonment. But she had quickly grown to like spending time with Matt, Naomi, and Joe. They treated her like a normal person, and she could use more of that type of treatment. Besides, she needed Matt to take her back to the clothes closet at the church.

The three continued their meals in silence. They all looked very tired and were preoccupied with their own thoughts. Mary came over to the table and refilled the mugs with coffee and poured more water for Sarah.

"Well ain't you guys a raucous bunch this morning." She snickered a little and laid the check on the table. "I hope everything is okay," she said, turning back to the table after starting to leave. "I haven't seen you guys this quiet in years."

Matt and Naomi waved their hands at her, and Sarah watched them. "Everything is good, Mary," Matt assured her. "We just had a heckuva day yesterday, and I think it has tuckered us all out."

"I suppose we all have those days," Mary replied, noticeably relieved.

As Matt walked to the counter to cover the check, Sarah whispered to Naomi, "Ummm … thanks for not saying anything."

"Honey, that is your secret to share, so I will not say anything," Naomi replied. "But I do caution you. Although he is a man and mostly oblivious to things like this, he is a preacher—and rather smart to boot."

Leaning closer to her as Matt made his way to them at the door, she added, "He might catch on quicker than you think." Sarah looked at Naomi, unsure of what to say.

"Who is going where and with whom?" Matt asked as he walked up to the ladies.

"I have my last day of school today," said Naomi. "Sarah, you are welcome to come with me because there is a good chance I will have exactly zero students in attendance today."

"Thanks," Sarah replied, "but I think I would like to look through the clothes closet at the church one more time."

"Alrighty," Matt said as he held the door open for the other two. "One to school and two to church." Then seeing Duke run out after the ladies, he added, "Make that three to church."

Matt drove Naomi to the high school and swung into the empty parking lot. "I believe you are right, Ms. Naomi," Matt remarked. "There is not hide nor hair of a student in this place."

Naomi laughed. "Summer fever is catching."

He pulled up to the door and let Naomi off at the curb. She jumped out and grabbed her bag from the back, giving Duke a pat on the head in the process. Naomi waved as she walked inside. Matt honked and Duke barked as the truck pulled away.

Leaving the parking lot, Matt noticed a familiar black Series 62 Cadillac nestled in the closest parking space to the school. The space was marked "Principal," but that was not the principal's car. The automobile belonged to none other than the Baron. Immediately, Matt felt sad for the principal, but relieved the Baron was not at the church.

Matt and Sarah, toting Duke in the back of the truck, drove the few blocks to the center of town and pulled into Matt's familiar space in front of the church. Duke jumped out of the back of the truck and landed on the sidewalk. He did not wait for the other two as he ran to the front doors of the church. Sarah grabbed her duffel from the back of the truck, and Matt offered to carry it to the entrance, but she declined.

"You know," Matt said, "you don't need to carry that thing everywhere. When you are ready to leave, we can grab it from wherever it may be."

"I feel better if it's with me," said Sarah.

"Suit yourself," Matt allowed as they made their way through the open door.

Albie stood at the end of the hallway with Matt's mug full of coffee. "Good morning, Preacher," she said with a big smile. "I am so happy to see you again, my girl Sarah," she said with even a bigger smile.

"Albie, you are a sight for sore eyes," Matt responded and graciously added, "Thank you so much for the coffee." Before Sarah could say anything, Albie had grabbed her in a giant bear hug. She hugged her and moved her from side to side.

"I am happy you are here again, Ms. Sarah. I have thought about you all night. It's a good sign that you are still here."

Sarah was unsure as to what she should say, but luckily, she could not say anything until Albie released her hold. As uncomfortable as she was, she also found the display of affection very pleasant and was content letting Albie hug her like she was a young bear cub.

"Albie, you better let her come up for air," Matt intervened.

"I know, I know," Albie said, letting go of Sarah. "You know how I get, though."

"Oh yes," Matt said giving a wide-eyed look at Sarah, "believe me, I know."

Knowing that Sarah wanted to look through the clothes closet again, he left her with Albie, and he went back to his office. Duke was already on his mat in the office, taking a morning nap. Obviously, Duke was also happy that the Baron had chosen to make other stops this morning.

It had only been hours since he had been in his office, but it felt like weeks. The meeting with the Baron the previous morning felt like decades ago. It was surreal to him that time could pass so quickly in one instance and so slowly in another.

He typically used Fridays to jot down some notes or talking points for his sermons on Sunday. It never really took long as he used no references and only hit the surface of most topics. He thought he might be able to knock out his next great sermon concerning working for others as working for God (like the Baron ordered) before lunch. Considering this topic was preached at least once a month, if not more, he pretty much had it down to a science.

Sarah and Albie sat in the break room while Albie enjoyed her own cup of coffee and Sarah worked her way through a sleeve of saltine crackers.

"Where you headed, my girl Sarah?" asked Albie.

"Mexico," Sarah replied, offering no further information.

"Seems to me that Mexico probably doesn't have the answers you are looking for, girl," Albie said as she sipped her coffee and looked over the brim of the cup at the young lady across from her. Sarah said nothing as she removed another cracker from the wrapper and bit into it.

"Seems to me that Mexico is where you go when you are running *from* something, not *to* something." Albie rested her cup on the table and leaned her head a little to one side, waiting for a response from Sarah.

Sarah refused to make eye contact with Albie and continued to look at the crackers as she fidgeted with the wrapping.

"I ain't here to lecture you though. Nope, not me," Albie continued, letting Sarah off the hook. She stood and carried her mug to the sink, quickly rinsed it out, and set it to the side. Sarah did not move a muscle, but watched Albie's every move.

"My girl Sarah, sometimes we just need to get out of our own way and let God work," Albie said with her back still to Sarah. Sarah looked up, and Albie turned around to say, "Get out of your own way, Sarah."

The phone started ringing at Albie's desk. She smiled at Sarah, held up her finger, and indicated she would be right back.

Albie picked up the phone and immediately lost her smile upon hearing the voice or the news on the other end. "Just one moment, and I will get him on the line for you," she said. She laid down the receiver and made her way to Matt's office. "Preacher, pick up the phone; there is an important call for you."

Albie alerted Matt after a few knocks on his door. She did not hear a response, so she opened the door and found Matt lost in his thoughts. Softly she began again, "Preacher, there is an important call for you. You need to pick up the phone."

Coming back from his dreams, Matt responded, "Oh … yes … okay … thank you, Albie." Reaching out for the phone receiver, Matt paused. "How is it going with Sarah?" Matt asked Albie.

Albie smiled. "Oh, I think I'm wearing her down."

"Good," said Matt. He took a deep breath and picked up the phone, saying, "This is Matt," expecting to hear the voice of the Baron on the other end. Instead he heard the voice of Paul Gentry.

"Matt, Millie died about an hour ago."

Chapter 16

Naomi opened the double glass doors to Central High School and made her way down the empty hallway to her room. She passed by the trophy case in the main hall and paused to look at some of the pictures of the sports teams over the years. Most of the faces she recognized and, happily, was able to recall the students' names. The sports teams from Central had never been part of the Texas elite, but there was the one year before the war that they had almost won the state championship.

She looked at the runners-up trophy—a mitt cradling a signed baseball—in the middle of the case. She examined the black-and-white picture of the team carefully and was saddened by the small annotations above several of the players: "Died in WW II." She was searching her memories when a hand touched her on the shoulder.

"Good morning, Naomi."

"Oh, good morning, Principal Hamilton," Naomi replied with a smile.

Principal Hamilton had been at Central High School for as long as Naomi cared to remember. He was a good administrator, a fair disciplinarian, and a superb educator. Naomi believed what made him superb was his attention to the students and his acknowledgment of their individual strengths.

It was not common for principals to take the time to know the individual students, but Principal Hamilton did just that in his school. Granted, in a small town it was easier to have personal relationships, but Naomi truly believed that the man cared about the welfare and future of every student who passed through his door.

"Naomi," Principal Hamilton said, looking somewhat despondent, "can you come with me to my office for a few minutes?" Naomi sensed that something was not right and silently agreed to follow the principal.

They walked the few steps to the office lobby where Janice, the secretary, mouthed, "Hello" to Naomi and held her hands up slightly above her desk with her fingers crossed. "Good luck," she mouthed as Principal Hamilton opened the door to his office.

Naomi stepped through the door the principal held open for her and was surprised to see two men rise from their seats when she entered. The first was easily recognizable with his tall, slender frame and his bushy moustache. "Miss Rhodes," the man said, nodding.

"Mr. Barrister," Naomi said, giving a slight nod back.

The second man held his hat in his hands at chest height. He was clearly uncomfortable in the setting, but was able to muster up a greeting as well: "Miss Rhodes."

Naomi took in a deep breath through her nose that filled up her chest with air; she let the breath go and replied to the man, "Good morning, Mr. Travis. I do hope that Peter is okay."

Mr. Travis looked at the floor, then quickly looked up. "Oh yes, ma'am, he is fine. We, uh, well … we—"

The Baron interrupted, "We believe you have overstepped your bounds with regards to Mr. Travis's young, impressionable son, Miss Rhodes."

Naomi felt her face go flush with the blood that was rising to the surface in her anger. She pointed her finger at the Baron and began to speak, but Principal Hamilton quickly intervened by saying, "Now, let's all sit down and discuss what has transpired here, without casting any blame on anyone."

The two men stood in front of their chairs at the small, round, wooden table in the office. Principal Hamilton pulled out a chair for Naomi, who took the seat, sat her bag on the floor beside the chair, and crossed her hands in front of her on the table.

The two men returned to their seats, and Principal Hamilton quickly sat in the last available seat. He tried to sit up straight in the chair, but was unable to get comfortable, and he fidgeted as he tried to decide where to put his hands. Nervously, he crossed, then uncrossed his legs. Finally, he pulled the chair close to the table and leaned forward on his forearms with his hands clasped in front of him.

"Mr. Travis," Principal Hamilton began, "please state for Miss Rhodes the complaint you have lodged against her this morning."

Peter Travis Sr. had one hand in his lap holding his hat and the other arm was stretched out on the table. He extended one of his fingers and tapped the table, then picked at some imaginary piece of matter on the table. His eyes were focused on his hand, but he would look up at Naomi every few seconds. The Baron cleared his throat, causing Mr. Travis to shift in his seat a little and pull the extended hand back to his lap. He glanced at the Baron, then at Naomi.

"Miss Rhodes, it seems you have filled my son's head with the idea he is going to the university," Mr. Travis finally said. "That, well, that just doesn't jive with the plans we had for Peter." Mr. Travis completed his statement and looked at the Baron for approval. The Baron provided a slight nod.

"I see," said Naomi in an even tone. She paused for a moment, but was clearly formulating her thoughts as a rebuttal. "Your son, Peter, is a remarkably intelligent and diligent young man," Naomi began. "He is an excellent candidate for higher education and can go far if he chooses to pursue that route and is given support from those around him."

She locked eyes directly with Peter's father and held them for a moment before releasing him from her last statement. Sensing the next line of attack that would be laid out against her, she charged on. "Peter is an excellent student and has performed well on the sports teams here at Central, while also contributing nicely to Mr. Barrister's factory. Therefore, his chances of receiving a scholarship covering the added expense of his education is highly probable."

She had stated the facts but decided to close on her emotions. "Peter is capable of larger and greater things than we can imagine for him. I encouraged him to find his own dreams and to pursue them."

The Baron slapped the table hard, and in a loud booming voice exclaimed, "Ah-ha! There you go, Principal, she admits to poisoning the young man against his father, his family, and against the factory."

"Now wait a minute, Mr. Barrister. I don't believe that is what she—" Principal Hamilton tried to counter, but was quickly cut off.

"She encouraged the young man to defy his parents by applying to college and potentially going against the family's plan for their son. Do you not admit to that being true?" He looked at Naomi and threw his hands in the air with his palms facing upward.

Mr. Travis had stretched his arm across the table again and continued to pick at the invisible spot. He did not look up. Naomi realized that the battle she was fighting was not against Mr. Travis or Peter's family, but against the Baron.

"I admit to encouraging Peter to Dukeimize his opportunities," she said while looking Jesse Barrister squarely in the eyes with resolve.

Again, Principal Hamilton tried to interject but was overrun by the Baron. "Dukeimizing opportunities, eh, Miss Rhodes?" the Baron said with a sneer on his face. "While their son is off at school for the next two to four years, the Travis family is losing the income their boy would be bringing in from a steady paying job."

He placed his hand on the shoulder of Mr. Travis and shook it like he cared deeply for the man. "Not only does that put more pressure on this man to feed his family at home, but now he has to care for his son and his son's expenses hours away. Is that Dukeimizing the family's potential, Miss Rhodes?"

Naomi began to respond, but the Baron continued, "You speak of the boy's intelligence and diligence. I agree. I have witnessed his work firsthand at Barrister Enterprises. He is going to move through our promotion system quickly, and I could see him as a foreman much faster than the average bird."

Mr. Travis raised his head and looked at the Baron. The other man pursed his lips and raised his eyebrows back at Mr. Travis. "That would be something, wouldn't it?" he said as an aside. Mr. Travis did not respond, but went back to focusing on the table.

Naomi had tried to be respectful and courteous to the men in the room, but she had hit her limit after witnessing the last exchange. "You three have obviously called me into this office to pressure me to tell Peter I was wrong, and that he should continue his work at the Baron's factory." All three men shifted uncomfortably, and they looked at each other with wide eyes when she used Mr. Barrister's nickname.

"Well, I won't!" she continued. "That boy, *your boy*, Mr. Travis," she said poking Mr. Travis's extended arm, "is a smart young man with the potential to do much more than work on a factory line the rest of his life."

She implored Mr. Travis to look at her. "Your son has hopes and dreams that go beyond the borders of this town, Mr. Travis.

He has the potential to succeed in achieving those dreams. Don't you want to at least let him try?" Mr. Travis never looked up, but moved his finger more quickly against the table.

"Well, Principal Hamilton," the Baron said in false exasperation, "I am not sure what kind of place you are running around here." Wagging his finger at Naomi, he said in a raised voice, "You bring this teacher in who turns a boy against his father, then in front of all of us, she disparages the man's livelihood as a factory worker."

"Mr. Barrister, Mr. Travis," Mr. Hamilton quickly responded while slightly waving his hands with the palms toward the table, "we all know that Miss Rhodes was not speaking against the work Mr. Travis does to support his family."

"I do not know that, Principal Hamilton," the Baron said as he gave the principal a hard stare. He sat back in his chair, grabbed the lapels of his sports jacket, and looked up at the ceiling.

Still examining the ceiling, he spoke. "Principal Hamilton, you have one of the best supplied schools in Texas. Your students have new books and all the laboratory equipment a high school could require." He changed his focus to Principal Hamilton and fixed his stare concretely on the principal's eyes.

"Your labs for vocational simulation are unsurpassed, I would venture to say, by any school in the nation." He pointed his long finger at the principal. "All of those instruct *your* students how to succeed in a factory that *your* prize teacher here seems to think is beneath a man's work."

Naomi countered with, "I want what is best for the children!"

"No, you want to fill their heads with mumbo jumbo and make them think their families are second-class citizens!" the Baron replied.

"Mr. Barrister, I believe you have misconstrued the intentions and thoughts of Miss Rhodes," Principal Hamilton interjected as he spoke in support of his teacher. "She is a passionate teacher who expects the best from her students in both academics and life. She cares about the children as if they are her own and encourages them to succeed."

The Baron removed a cigar from the inner pocket of his coat. He rolled it in his fingers for a moment, looking at it, then used it to point at the principal. "You should take a moment to carefully choose which side of this discussion you are on. It would be very difficult to maintain such a nice facility if you were to lose funding."

And there it was. The Baron had pulled out his trump card and now aimed to wield the power he held over the principal.

"This is what is going to happen," the Baron said, leaning forward, clenching his unlit cigar in his teeth. "Miss Rhodes here, is going to tell young Peter that she was wrong and that the factory provides grand opportunity. Then she is going to apologize to the Travis family. Then she is going to apologize to me." He sat back in his chair and crossed his legs.

"And if that does not happen?" Mr. Hamilton questioned.

"Well, it is your choice." The Baron shrugged. "You can lose your funding or you can terminate Miss Rhodes." Naomi stood. Principal Hamilton and Mr. Travis stood as well. The Baron remained seated with his legs crossed and chewing on his cigar.

"I refuse," said Naomi. She knew what this meant, so she looked at Principal Hamilton and took his hand. "It's okay," she assured her friend, "retirement is a glorious opportunity." She looked at Mr. Travis and smiled at him to let him know that this was not his fault, for she knew this meeting was likely not his doing. Mr. Travis provided a thin smile back and seemingly issued an apology with the expression in his eyes.

Finally, the Baron stood. "We simply can't have folks speaking against our investments, Miss Rhodes. It is bad business."

Naomi gathered her bag and left the office. Obviously the heated exchange had filtered into the outer office, and Janice sat at her desk with tears in her eyes. She dabbed at them with a tissue as Naomi entered the room.

Janice rose from her seat and wrapped her arms around Naomi. "It is not fair," she said.

Naomi tried not to join in the tears when she replied, "Oh, it's okay. It is time for me to move on." The two moved apart from their embrace, and Naomi exited the office.

She thought about going to her classroom, but decided now was not the time. She turned right and walked past the large trophy case for, what was likely, the last time. When she reached the outer doors, she pushed one open and stepped through, looking back down the hallway and envisioning all of the students she had taught over her lifetime filling the empty corridor. They waved good-bye to her as she stepped across the metal threshold into the bright June sun.

Chapter 17

Albie returned to the break room and opened the icebox. She removed a glass bowl half full of pimento cheese spread and a loaf of bread and set it on the table. Sarah watched as Albie worked quickly to spread the cheese on the bread and form a sandwich. She tore off a piece of parchment paper from a nearby roll and wrapped the sandwich, folding the paper so a single point fell in the center of the sandwich. She closed the paper with a piece of tape.

Albie pulled a brown paper bag from a drawer next to the icebox and an apple from a bowl on the table. She threw the apple in the bag and placed the sandwich on top. She rolled down the top of the bag two or three times to secure its contents. Just then, Matt came into the room, followed by his furry, four-legged shadow.

Matt spoke quietly, "Albie, I need to go to the Gentrys' house. Would it be all right if Sarah and Duke were to stay with you?"

"You do what you need to do, Preacher," replied Albie, handing Matt the brown bag. "Me and Sarah got this place covered." Then she looked at Duke. "I'll watch that rascal too."

Matt nodded in appreciation and smiled at Sarah and patted Duke on the head, then slowly turned and left. Albie quickly placed some of the spread on a saltine and tossed it to Duke, who caught it in the air. Albie took her right hand and raised it to her face, placing two of the fingers near her eyes, and then she pointed at Duke with her index finger, indicating she was watching him. Duke turned his head to one side, then lay down on his front paws with a grunt. Sarah and Albie both laughed.

Sarah asked Albie, "How did you know he was going to need that sandwich?"

"Oh, child," Albie said with a wave of her hand, "there are some calls that just have to be answered in person. The Lord is working on our dear preacher, yes sirree." Albie smiled. "Just like He is working on you." Sarah shook her head and looked at the floor.

"Tell me, girl," Albie continued, "what do you think about the Man upstairs?"

Sarah looked around the room, then at Duke. He kept his head on his paws and looked up at her through the top of his eyes.

"It is not a hard question, my girl," continued Albie. Sarah was very uncomfortable, and she shifted in her seat, actually making herself more uncomfortable in the process.

"I used to pray," she said softly.

"Ah, that means you know God, huh child?" Albie asked. Sarah nodded slightly. She looked at Albie, and Albie flashed her a toothy grin.

"Tell me more, Sarah. Why'd you stop praying?"

Sarah said nothing. She no longer looked at Albie, but looked at the floor. She straightened her left arm across the table, than laid her head on the arm, looking away from Albie.

Seeing that she would not get any answers from Sarah, Albie thought it would be nice to share some of her own story.

"Young Sarah, do you know how old I am?" There was no movement from the girl. "Well, let me tell you," Albie continued. "I am forty-five years old, born in April of 1917." She leaned back against the cabinets lining the wall.

"People think I am older than that because my skin is rough, and my face is wrinkled." She held her hands out in front of herself and examined them as she spoke. "But a life of hard work takes a toll on the body, girl, mmmm-huh.

"You see, child," Albie said, making her way to the side of the room Sarah was facing, "me and mine did not have anything to our names."

Then she added, "We hadn't even had our names for very long. Oh, child, so I prayed. I prayed every night that we would have a big house and pretty clothes and great big feasts and parties." Albie moved her hands and swayed to the sound of imaginary music. "We never did have those things though, Sarah."

Albie stopped smiling. "I thought that meant God favored others over me and mines." She shrugged. "So there was no use praying if God wasn't listening."

Sarah was sitting up and looking at Albie now. The older woman looked her in the eyes, and Sarah could see the compassion behind her gaze. "I took a Saturday job after my last boy was born, sometime before the war, and cleaned the church here once a week." She laughed at the recollection.

"Preacher Matt was a different man back then. He was young and full of the Spirit, and he wanted everybody else to be too."

Albie pointed over at the main sanctuary building through the wall. "I was cleaning the pews in there one Saturday, and he came up from behind and scared the boogie-woogie out of me." Her face scrunched together. "He claimed he had never seen me smile, and he wondered why. I sat there much like you are with me today and said nothing." She poked Sarah's shoulder. "Then he asked me the same question I just asked you."

She looked at Sarah with her eyebrows raised. "You know what I said?" Sarah shook her head. "I said exactly what you said: 'I used to,'" Albie responded. "Oh we sat and we talked in that church for hours. Finally my husband, God rest his soul, came through the doors looking for me."

She grabbed Sarah's hand. "You see, girl, time had stopped for me because I found my faith in God again. My prayers had been all about what I thought I wanted, not about what God had given me. I felt cheated, but to tell the truth, my life was abundant."

Her face shone with the biggest smile Sarah had ever seen. "It is hard to see the love amidst the mess, but when you start looking for it, you can't help but to see it."

"What did he tell you that day?" asked Sarah.

"Child, I wish I knew. I cannot remember. Don't suppose I need to remember, really," Albie said in her typical jovial fashion, allowing the omission to have very little impact.

Sarah looked at Albie and wanted to offer her a sign of understanding and appreciation, but she still was prevented from doing so. She was certain that Albie just did not understand how hard her life had been and how unfairly God—if there even was a God—had treated her.

Sure, Sarah thought to herself, *she can talk about love all she wants, but God doesn't even like me.* She wrung her hands in front of herself. *How could He love me, especially after the things I have done? Plus, my mom didn't even want me.* At that point, her feelings grew cold toward Albie's story, and she was ready to leave.

"Albie," she said abruptly, "can you let me in the clothes closet again?" She moved her head in the direction of her duffel bag. "Some of the things from yesterday didn't fit, and I wanted to see what else I could find."

Albie, somewhat disappointed in the response, did not push the young girl. "Sure, my girl, sure." They both stood, followed by Duke. Sarah grabbed her duffel bag, and the three made their way through the maze of cubicles back to the clothes closet again.

Albie pulled out her keys and unlocked the padlock on the door. She opened the door and let Sarah in. Albie grabbed Sarah by both shoulders and looked straight in her eyes. "Don't you harden your heart, girl. You let God do His work on you, and you will be just fine." She gave her a smile and a nod for emphasis. "Just lock it back up when you're done, and c'mon back out front."

Sarah watched as Albie and Duke walked away, making their way back to her desk. She was sorry she had not responded better to Albie's story, because she knew that Albie was really trying to help her. But she could not be sidetracked, and there was no more time to talk.

She went into the clothes closet and grabbed the string hanging from the ceiling; the bare lightbulb came on to brighten the room. She looked outside the door one more time and slowly closed it behind her. Setting her duffel bag on the floor, she pulled out some of the clothes she had selected the day before and placed them on the bag. Then Sarah made her way to the wall nearest the door that was stocked with handbags and other accessories. She found a medium-size leather handbag that opened wide at the top and closed with a leather strap and buckle. "This should work," she said to herself.

At a rapid pace, she moved through the rack of clothes to the far side of the room beside the wall, then walked down the aisle until she came to the donation box against the wall. From the inside of her jacket, she pulled out a wrapped napkin. When Sarah unrolled the napkin, it revealed a knife she had taken from the Blossom Dairy earlier that morning.

She looked back over the racks of clothes to ensure the door was still shut, then inserted the knife between the wire connections of the small padlock security of the donation box. She began to twist the knife quickly. The pressure extended the wires and caused them to wrap around each other with each twist. After only four turns, there was a *pop*, and the lock was free from the box.

Sarah grabbed the handbag and placed it below the box, opening it as wide as it would go. Holding the strap of the bag out of the way, she wrapped her free hand around the handle on the bottom of the box and pulled it toward her. The box opened with a slight *creak*—and nothing came out.

She frantically reached inside the box thinking that the money and coins must have been hung up on something. Nothing was there except some chewing gum stuck to the sides of the box. She violently pushed the bag out of the way and got down on her hands and knees and looked up into the box. There was sunlight coming through the opening on the outside, revealing what she already knew: the box was empty.

Sarah wanted to scream, but instead sat with her back against the wall, held her hands to her face, and began to cry.

Chapter 18

Matt slowed his truck to a stop in front of the white fence at the Gentrys' home. He had hoped to have a moment to gather his thoughts before making his way through the gate and to the house, but a partially raised hand slowly moving back and forth revealed that he had been seen by Paul Gentry, sitting in a rocking chair on the porch.

He took a deep breath and held it for a moment, then looked at himself in the rearview mirror. Matt did not like the tired, old man he saw, so he tilted the mirror away and opened the door. He made his way to the gate, and as he walked through, he waved. "Hello, Paul."

"Hi, Matt," Paul said with a genuine gladness to see the preacher in his voice. "Forgive me for not standing; I am just a bit tired."

Matt made his way across the porch to the corner where Paul sat. There was an open rocker beside Paul with a wicker table in between. Oddly, there was a wrapped package on the table.

Paul and Millie could be seen most mornings and evenings sitting in these chairs, drinking cool iced teas in the summer and steaming coffees in the fall. As folks walked past the Gentry house, the couple would wave and call out to them by name. They were loved by the town and bore the image of the way life used to be before the war had confused things.

Matt motioned toward the chair. "May I?" he asked. Paul, thankful for Matt's consideration, nodded. Matt took his seat beside Paul, and the two men sat in silence and surveyed the street in front of them for a long time before Paul broke the quiet.

"Every day for the last eighteen years, I have asked God why He took my son," Paul said, still looking out over the street. "I have never received an answer or an inclination," he continued. "But I knew every time I asked the question, there was a father somewhere else asking the same question at the same time."

Glancing at Matt, he told him, "It is very hard, you know, losing a child … well, I suppose he was a man, but still, he was my boy." He looked down at his hands in his lap. "I just never knew why it had to happen, until now."

"What do you mean?" Matt asked.

"Matt, my Millie was certain that Billy would be waiting for her when the time came for her to move on. Last night, she had an awful fit and could not catch her breath." Tears were now welling up in Paul's eyes and rolling down his pale cheeks.

"I wanted to call the doctor, but she grabbed my hand and looked at me … I mean, her eyes … she was telling me it was time."

Then he paused and looked at Matt. "Isn't it a wonder how eyes can convey so much meaning without a word being spoken?" Matt nodded. "Anyway," Paul continued, "she clutched my hand, and her fit seemed to subside, but her breathing was shallow and erratic." He held his hands to his face and put his elbows on his knees. "I couldn't take it—I just couldn't take it. So I phoned the doctor and asked him to come.

"When I returned to the room," he said as he sat back up in the chair and looked at Matt, "she was so peaceful. Her eyes were open, and she had a smile on her face, Matt. It was a big smile, and her eyes showed so much joy. Our Billy took his mama home," Paul said as he finally broke down in tears.

Matt placed his hand on Paul's back as the man wept for the loss of his wife and the happiness of her reunion with their son after so many years apart.

Paul had been holding on to the emotions of his loss since the moment Millie passed, and he was relieved to have the opportunity to let them out as his friend offered comfort. He had always considered Matt a friend and had believed that it was God who placed Matt with Billy as his son died. Although it had never been spoken between them, Paul knew what he considered to be a blessing, Matt considered a curse.

He sat up in his chair and stretched his arm over Matt's and patted Matt on the back. Matt returned the action to Paul. Paul nodded his appreciation, and Matt smiled. The two men released their hold and sat back in their chairs.

Matt had so many things he wished to convey to Paul right now, but he simply was not able to. What Paul had said regarding Millie's final moments had surprised Matt, and he hoped that his expression had not shown his surprise or hinted at his disbelief.

How could the son have been so scared, while the mother had been so content? Billy had wanted so desperately to see God in his final moments, but he was not offered the comfort, or so it seemed. Could it be possible that Paul was right, and Billy ushered his mother into the kingdom of heaven? Matt was struggling to find truth in the events of the past and in the events of the present.

Paul gently slapped Matt on his knee. Matt leaned forward and shifted his attention to Paul. The older man reached down to the table and picked up the package wrapped in silver paper and a green bow. He laughed a bit as he handed it to Matt. "Millie was very upset that we only had Christmas paper in the house."

Matt was surprised. "What is it, Paul?"

"It is for you, Matt," Paul responded with a smile. "We have had it for a long time, and it's time it came back to you."

Matt sat in disbelief. "I am not sure what to say," he said.

Paul took a deep breath. "Matt, you are going to be stunned most likely when you open that package. So, I am not going to say much. In fact, you might want to open it when you are somewhere else."

Paul leaned forward and clasped his hands in front of him with his elbows on his knees. "Millie took the time to wrap it up and write you a note when she knew that this day was coming." His look at Matt conveyed compassion, thankfulness, forgiveness, and empathy all in one expression.

"Wow, Paul, I just … I am … I don't know what to say." Matt shrugged as words escaped him. "I want to open it here, with you, if that's okay," he said.

"Thank you for that," Paul replied. He had been hoping that would be the result.

Matt nodded and looked down at the package he held in his lap. He glanced at Paul, then gently pulled at the green ribbon. The ribbon came free from the packaging, and Matt placed it on the table. He held the package in his right hand and slid his left fingers under the crease in the paper. The paper pulled away from the box that it disguised, and Matt folded the paper quickly and placed it on the table beside the bow.

An ordinary shirt box now sat on Matt's lap. He felt excitement and dread as to what the contents of the box may be, but most of all, he felt curiosity. With hands on either side, he removed the lid of the box. Sitting on top of tissue paper was a sealed envelope, likely containing the letter Paul had indicated. It simply read, "Preacher," in Millie's handwriting.

Paul put his hand on Matt's shoulder. "You can read that later, Matt." Paul moved in closer, almost hanging over the open box, waiting for Matt to reveal the hidden contents. Matt gave a slight shake of his head and pulled back the tissue paper. His eyes became moist as he looked upon the Bible he had left on the beach beside Billy Gentry almost twenty years ago.

Matt was afraid to touch the book. He stared at its rugged cover that was surrounded by the softness and beauty of the wrapping.

Paul watched Matt process what sat before him. In an effort to soften the blow, he said, "Matt, when Billy was brought back to us from overseas, we were given a box of his belongings. Among the things in the box was your Bible." He sat back in his chair and began rocking while Matt looked at Paul, still a bit dazed.

"Oh we always intended to give it back to you, Matt," Paul continued, "but it became this connection between us and Billy's last moments on earth. It just got harder and harder to give it back, and then, well, it seemed wrong to give it back after so much time had gone by."

Matt followed Paul's logic and nodded in understanding. "It's okay, Paul ... you can keep it if you want or need—"

"No," Paul interrupted. "It has been with Millie and me for long enough—maybe even too long. You need it now." He looked at his watch and sighed. "I have to go to the funeral parlor."

"You want me to go with you?" Matt asked.

"No," said Paul, "that's all right. I figure it is picking out things and signing paperwork and writing a check." Then he added as a realization, "Probably a good business in death." The men stood from their rockers and moved to the stairs on the porch. They held out their right hands and shook hands warmly.

"I would like to know," began Paul, "what Psalm was it that you spoke to Billy as he was dying."

Matt was thrown by the question, and it took him a moment to respond, "Psalm 27 ... well, parts of it anyway."

Paul snapped his fingers and pointed at Matt. "I knew it. Only parts though, huh?" He wagged his finger at Matt. "You, my friend, should read the whole thing." Paul opened the door behind him and made his way into the house as Matt started down the steps.

Abruptly, Matt stopped and turned toward the door and called, "Paul!" Paul came to the screen door. "How did you know it was Psalm 27?" Matt asked.

Paul looked at the ground. "It was the page with the bloodstains." Then he turned and disappeared into the house.

Chapter 19

Sarah held the busted wire lock in her hand and sat, unsure of her next move. There was no way to replace the lock on the box and to restore its broken connections. She had not anticipated the need to put things back together. So she decided simply to put the busted lock in her bag and leave the donation box in its unlocked condition. It would probably be at least a few days before anyone noticed, especially if it had just been emptied.

She wiped her eyes on her sleeves and began pushing clothes back into her duffel bag. She threw the lock in the bag among the clothes and pushed the clothes tightly down into the back. There was no way the lock would come out and expose her botched robbery attempt. Then Sarah placed the handbag back onto the shelf so as not to raise any suspicion of her need for carrying the new accessory.

After taking a quick glance around the room, Sarah pulled her fingers through her hair and made her way to the door. The door opened slightly with her push, and she was able to fit her head in the space between the frame and the door. Peeking into the adjacent room and then down the hallway, she decided the coast was clear, so no one had seen a thing! With relief, she started out into the room. She half expected Albie to be standing behind the door saying, "Gotcha, mmmm-huh," as she closed the door behind her, but no one was there.

Her walk back to the front of the building was quick and deliberate. She was startled as she emerged from the back hallway into the lighted office area because she was greeted with a flash of fur and two paws on her midsection.

"Oh, Duke! You scared me! Get down!" Duke sat on the floor in front of her and lowered his head. Sarah felt bad she had yelled at him, and his expression certainly did not make her feel any better, so she knelt down, placing her duffel bag by her side.

Sarah cupped Duke's face in her hands. "Aww, you're a good boy, Duke. You just caught me off guard, that's all." She scratched his head, and he showed his forgiveness by dancing back and forth on his front paws and wagging his tail. She snickered and told him, "Silly dog," then picked up her bag and continued on to Albie's desk.

Albie was not at her desk, but Sarah heard her singing in the break room. She was working on a project on the side counter, and when Sarah walked into the room, quit singing. Pausing in her work, she then turned and faced Sarah with a welcoming smile. "Did you find what you were looking for, sugar?" asked Albie.

Sarah shook her head. "Naw. I had trouble finding stuff that fit me right."

"Well, I suppose that is the problem with shopping in the closet; you just don't know what you'll find in the right size," responded Albie.

Sarah stood in front of Albie and was unsure as to whether she should sit down or possibly turn and run. Albie smiled a wide smile at Sarah, which made Sarah comfortable enough to take a seat at the break table.

"My girl Sarah, let me tell you something," Albie began. "My kids are almost all grown." She sat down beside Sarah. "They are good kids, and they come back often to look in on their mama."

Recollecting her family's hardships, she added, "They grew up in some tough times … Their daddy died young, and people treated them bad because of the color of their skin."

Albie looked at the table for a brief moment and collected her thoughts. Determined in her approach, she said, "They had it rough, but we were family and together we overcame the bad stuff."

She motioned upward with her hands. "We kept our focus on God and worked hard to keep Him in our sights. Oh child, now you believe me when I tell you there were times when I wanted to beat someone, or even to run away from it all. But I couldn't."

She grabbed Sarah's hand and told her, "My family would not let me do anything that took me further from them." Albie stood and walked over to the counter where she had been working. Sarah said nothing, but followed Albie with her eyes as she moved.

"I am not sure where your family is, my girl Sarah," Albie said with her back to Sarah, "and I don't know what happened that has brought you here." She turned around quickly. "And it makes no never mind anyway." She paused for a second to see if Sarah would respond in any way.

When she did not, Albie held her arms out wide and lovingly said, "My girl Sarah, what I am trying to say to you is that my family could be your family. I think God would be happy if you came to stay with us for a while."

Sarah's eyes filled with tears, and her heart begged her to say yes. It felt good to be wanted and to be cared for. She had not expected it after her arrival at the diner the day before, but she had received nothing but kindness and compassion from Naomi, Matt, Joe, and Albie. Now, she was even being offered a place to stay and the chance to be part of a family. But, she concluded, Albie doesn't know.

If she knew, Sarah thought, *she would not even let me in this break room with her right now.* She stood from her seat and said,

"No, Albie, I can't. It is not that I … It's just that I can't, Albie. I can't."

Albie moved across the room to where Sarah was standing, "My girl Sarah." She wrapped her arms around Sarah and pulled the girl closer in her comforting grasp. Tears came down Sarah's cheeks, and she nestled her head between Albie's neck and shoulder.

"You just don't know me, Ms. Albie," Sarah said softly.

"My girl, I know you," replied Albie, "because God knows you, and God loves you. You and me—we are sisters, and I know you."

Albie pulled an envelope out of her dress pocket. "Sometimes, my girl, we try to handle things because we think God isn't with us or He isn't paying us, no never mind," Albie said, waving the envelope at Sarah. "The truth is, my girl, He has given us everything we need; we just have got to get ourselves out of the way so we can see it."

She placed the envelope on the table in front of Sarah. "Like I said to you earlier, my girl, get yourself out of your own way." Albie placed her hand on Sarah's shoulder and began to walk out of the room.

Stopping before she exited the room, Albie turned with a smile to Sarah and then nodded toward the envelope. "It is not stealing if it was yours all along."

Sarah quickly picked up the envelope and broke the seal, revealing many green bills of various amounts. She turned toward the door, but Albie was gone.

Joe could hardly recollect his drive back from Austin. He had enjoyed having his window rolled down as he smoked from his pipe nearly the whole trip. He tried to not make a habit of smoking in the car, but he was in a celebratory mood. In his thoughts, he kept reliving the moment he had swung his legs over the wall and viewed the beautiful rooftop garden.

He had thought that the one thing he was able to pass down to his son was not wanted, but what Joe was shown was quite the contrary. His son was a better farmer than he was.

"Anyone can grow crops in a field," Joe said aloud, "but on a big-city rooftop! Now that takes talent!" He laughed and slapped the steering wheel. He only had a short drive left, and he could not wait to share his celebration with Naomi.

Taking the pipe from his mouth, he ran his finger across the smooth cherrywood of the finely made smoker. He and Annie had spied the pipe in a window only days before he had enlisted in the war effort. He remembered turning to Annie and saying to her, "Someday, when all of this settles down, we will be sitting by the fire watching our children play on the floor."

She had seemed thrilled at the idea and giggled as he painted the picture more vibrantly. "You will be knitting in your rocking chair, and I will be reading the paper and"—he pointed through the window—"smoking that pipe." They both laughed and continued walking hand-in-hand down the street.

Joe had just finished basic training and had arrived for duty when he received a package from Annie. He tore through the brown paper and revealed a small box. Opening the box, he was shocked to see a handkerchief embroidered with the word, "Dad," wrapped around the cherry pipe he had admired in the window a month before.

Inside the bowl of the pipe was a small, rolled piece of paper. Joe removed the paper and gently unfurled it to reveal the short message: "Hurry home, Daddy." How he wished he could have held Annie at that moment. How he wished she could have seen how happy he was.

He felt happy driving back from his visit with Joseph as well. They had been through so much together, and Joe had tried to hide his insecurities of being a single father in a rough exterior. He felt guilty for not being there when Annie died. He felt he had let her and Joseph down by not being there to protect them.

But as the highway lines passed quickly beneath the car, he began to realize that, after the tragedy, his guilt and his own self-loathing had caused his vision of his blessings to be obscured.

~~∞∞∞~~

Naomi had been walking around town the better part of the afternoon until finally making her way back to her house. She ascended the steps and opened the screen door with a creak and the front door with a push. She let her bag drop to the living room floor with a thud and made her way to the kitchen. Even though she was hot from walking in the early summer heat, she filled the teapot with tap water and placed it on the stove to heat.

As she was waiting on the teapot to whistle, she made her way back to the porch and kicked her shoes off at the mat. She sat in the swing and listened to the birds and insect sounds around her. There was a slight breeze that blew coolly across her face and caused her hair to blow against her ears and neck.

Naomi was taken back to her class only the day before where Peter had asked about Lieutenant Henry. She laughed a bit at the irony of the question now. The lieutenant had stood in the middle of a street in an unfamiliar place, without any clues as to what was to happen in his life. He had so hoped for it to turn out a certain way, but it turned out very differently.

Naomi empathized with Lieutenant Henry in that moment more than she cared to as she gently pushed down on her toes, causing her to gently sway back and forth in the swing. Perhaps even greater than the irony of the day's events was that, just like the lieutenant, her destiny had been changed by a mother's death in childbirth. She breathed in deeply and was startled awake from her daydreams by the sound of the whistling teapot in her kitchen.

Chapter 20

Matt sat in the driver's seat of his truck and held the closed box in his lap, staring at the blank, white top that shielded the surprising contents from his view. His feelings upon opening the box were conflicted. At first, it was as if he had found something that had long been lost, but not forgotten.

Then, he remembered that it had not been lost, but left behind. It was not something he considered precious, but instead, it was a reminder of a time where all in which he had faith crumbled. It was remarkable to him, however, that all of these years later, it returned to him from the place where he abandoned it thousands of miles away.

His thoughts turned to Millie. He pictured her thumbing through the pages and coming across the pages with her son's smeared, bloody fingerprints immortalized as if they were a strange work of art. Could she have been comforted to know in his last moments his thoughts were with God, or was she appalled or angered by the blood spilled by men grasping for power? Perhaps the answer was both. Matt knew that the answer to his contemplations lay in an envelope in the box on his lap.

Matt tapped the box with his fingers and rested his head back against the rear window of his truck. His thoughts raced between a time long past and the present. The familiar prickly sensation started in his neck, and the blackness began to creep into his peripheral vision. He removed his hat and sat it on the passenger seat and breathed in deeply through his mouth. His chest tightened, and his mouth became dry. His hands gripped the steering wheel tighter and tighter until his knuckles and fingers were white from the pressure.

He was startled by a honk from a car as Paul Gentry pulled from his driveway and drove toward the funeral home to handle the unpleasant task of burying his wife. Matt mustered his best, encouraging face and gave a wave of his hand. Paul's brown Ford moved slowly down the road in front of him.

Matt tried to concentrate on his breathing, and he began to recite the psalm he had recited so many times before: "The Lord is my shepherd, I shall not want. He maketh me …" Matt became lost. He could not remember the next words, and his emotions seized him in a panic.

His memories discharged on him like a rapid-fire machine gun. Each image slammed against his soul like a slug from a large caliber rifle. As a young boy, he was dressed all in white and was raised from the water, allowing it to fall freely from his head, and he smiled as he opened his eyes.

His mother and father smiled as he was ordained by the church and presented to the congregation. He looked in the mirror at himself in a US Army uniform. Then there were explosions and screams. Men hollered for Matt and waved him down to bring him over to their friends in need.

His body jerked as each bomb exploded in his mind. Tears came down his cheeks as he visited wounded and lifeless soldier after soldier. His hand pounded the steering wheel with such force that he felt a shooting pain travel up his arm each time his hand landed.

Matt tried to breathe deeply and to regain control, but he was trapped in the spiraling dark funnel of past memories and the horror of impending death. His throat tightened, and his chest throbbed with pain. Every nerve in his body seemed to fire continuously as if prodded by some source of electricity. Perspiration mixed with his tears, and he could taste the saltiness of the fluids as they rolled across his lips.

As he struggled to keep his eyes open, the blackness extended through the periphery and covered his field of view. All he could see was the past, and it held him captive. In seeing the past, he dreaded the future.

He stiffened as he saw Billy standing before him in his army fatigues. There was blood and sand covering the young man's attire, and his face was black from charred skin and gunpowder. The young man reached out toward Matt, and Matt screamed in his truck, "I'm sorry, Billy." Matt sobbed hard and fell weakly against his arms, which were held in place by the steering wheel—"I am so, so sorry."

Billy stood before him, still reaching out, but then he lowered his arm. His face became clear and free from the dirt and the wounds. The blood on his uniform began to fade, and the sand fell away from the fabric. Behind Billy, a great light shone, and it enveloped him until he was only a silhouette.

Matt's breathing slowed, and his muscles began to relax. The stinging sensations that plagued his nerves began to subside, and he grimaced occasionally as a stinger moved through an arm or his neck. As he breathed deeply and put his hands on his head, this allowed more air to fill his lungs. He closed his eyes and concentrated on the rising and lowering of his chest.

He pictured Millie lying peacefully in her bed with the gentle smile on her face. She slowly raised her hand, and it was met by another, much younger hand. Millie opened her eyes and smiled as she rose from the bed and fell into the arms of her young son. Matt gasped and opened his eyes. There was stillness in the truck; his breathing had returned to a slow and steady rhythm.

After several moments, he opened the glove compartment and removed a pack of fresh handkerchiefs. Sliding his hand between the edges of the wrapping, he broke the seal and removed one of the handkerchiefs. He unfolded it and tossed the pack onto the seat beside him.

Then Matt placed his face in the open cloth held in the palm of his hands and moved it forward over the top of his head. Then folding the cloth in half, he wiped his neck from both directions. His skin immediately cooled as the handkerchief absorbed the accumulated perspiration from his skin.

He sighed deeply and dabbed at his mouth with the cloth. His hands found the box, which had remained on his lap through the ordeal. Unwilling to completely reveal the contents of the box, he opened one side and slid his hand over the tissue paper until he found what he was looking for.

Slowly Matt pulled the envelope from the box and lowered the cover. He placed it on the box and stared at it for a moment, wondering what truth the letter within it would reveal.

Wiping his face and his eyes one more time with the handkerchief, Matt then balled the fabric in his hand as he reached for the envelope. He started at the upper corner of the envelope and then gently and slowly tore the paper open down the side so as to not harm the paper inside. Tearing the side completely off, he held the envelope to his mouth and blew into it while applying pressure on the sides.

The envelope opened to reveal a single piece of stationery folded twice. Matt removed the paper and set the envelope on top of his hat in the passenger's seat. He took a deep breath and unfolded the stationery.

The stationery was a simple design with a rhododendron blossom in the corner. A capital *G* was embossed in gold atop the bloom. There was no date on the letter, but given the contents of the package, Matt assumed it had been written recently. Matt's eyes found the first words written in Millie's flowing script in blue ink.

Dear Preacher Matt,

I am finally returning something that belongs to you. I apologize for keeping it so long, but it provided me wonderful warmth amidst the coldness the loss of our boy had brought. After a few months, we really did not even need the Bible because we had memorized the words on the pages stained with the colors of battle. But having the Bible comforted me, and knowing my Billy had touched it in his last moments allowed me to hold him close to my chest.

I have always taken great relief in knowing that God allowed you to be with my Billy when he died. What a miracle it truly was that in his time of need, so far from home, God sent him you to provide peace in a hectic place. Even though I was so angry for so long, I found my own peace in the love God showed in that act.

Paul and I noticed that you have not carried a Bible since coming home. I hope you will now see fit to do otherwise. You have struggled, but God has not let you fall. The words of the book I am returning tell that story over and over. Just as I found peace by clinging to this book, I hope you can find the strength to allow yourself to trust in God again.

You saved my boy by showing him love in his final moments on earth. Please take this Bible back as my attempt to show love to you in my final moments on earth.

Warmest regards,

Millie Gentry

P.S. Please look in on my Paul from time to time.

Matt looked up from the letter and gazed through the front windshield of his truck. His emotions were still raw from his episode only moments earlier, and he used the handkerchief to wipe away the tears from his face. He gently folded the letter up from the bottom and then slowly folded the top of the letter down, hiding the bloom of the rhododendron between the folds.

Then Matt reached over and found the envelope and slid the letter back into its sleeve for safekeeping. Lifting a corner of the box, he placed the letter back inside, then closed the box. He exchanged the box for his hat on the passenger's seat.

Placing his hat upon his head, he started the engine of the truck. Breathing in, he felt no constriction in his lungs or his chest. He took a deep breath and shook his head slightly as he pulled from the curb.

Chapter 21

Joe arrived at Naomi's house just after five o'clock in the evening. He turned the wheel and directed the car into her drive, and he saw her sitting on the porch. He clenched his pipe in his teeth and waved to her out his window. As Joe came to a stop, he playfully honked on the horn to accentuate his arrival. Naomi smiled and waved back at him, laughing at his theatrics.

Joe reached into his breast pocket and removed the handkerchief that safeguarded his pipe. Standing beside the car, he hit the pipe on his palm to remove the remaining tobacco. Once he was sure it was clear, he wrapped it carefully, but quickly, in the handkerchief. He did not want to pause to accomplish this task, but Naomi did not like his smoking and would have made him stow the pipe regardless of his own desire.

He moved up the walk with a certain spring in his step that made Naomi laugh out loud. "Well, I would say that someone had a very good trip!" exclaimed Naomi.

"Yes, indeedee," replied Joe. "You could certainly say that." He bounded up the steps and walked over to Naomi on the swing. He removed his hat and held it to his chest as he bent down and kissed her gently on the cheek.

"Hello, Naomi." Joe said with a smile. Naomi blushed.

"May I?" asked Joe while motioning to the open seat beside Naomi on the swing. She nodded and raised her hands to her hair as if she was trying to make sure it was in place.

She turned to Joe as he sat down. "Tell me, Joe, what happened? From your mood, I can only guess that Joseph has agreed to come back to the farm." Then she opened her mouth and gasped, "*Joe!* You didn't guilt that poor boy to come back and work here in this godforsaken town on that farm?"

Joe held up his hands in defense. "Hey, hey, easy on the old man now." He laughed. "No, Joseph will not be coming back to this old town and that old farm," Joe said, playing with the hat he held in his hands.

Naomi gave Joe a look of bewilderment. For as long as she could remember, the only thing the man who shared the swing with her wanted was for his son to take over the farm. His joy seemed misplaced when combined with the revelation he had shared. Yet, here he sat smiling and looking out at the street over the railing of her porch.

"I'm not sure I understand," Naomi said quietly.

From the time he had entered his car in Austin to the time he pulled in Naomi's drive, Joe had rehearsed the speech he was about to give. His nerves sought to betray him, but he took a deep breath and spoke softly and deliberately.

"Joseph is the director of the boys and girls home in Austin," Joe started.

Naomi smiled and slapped her knee. "Well of all the secrets …"

"I was very surprised myself," said Joe. "The place is magnificent," he continued. "There were children of all ages coming and going from the building. They played games and jumped rope, singing songs." He offered Naomi a proud smile. "Those children were so happy."

Joe ran his fingers around the brim of his hat. "I have been so selfish in my life, Naomi." He changed his tone. "I thought the only thing I could give my son was the farm, and the crops that had been given to me."

He shook his head slightly. "I have always been a gruff man, but that boy, well, he has always melted my heart, and I wanted to give him all that I could."

He fixed his eyes on Naomi's eyes. "But, I could never grasp that he did not want what I had to give, until today." His eyes became glassy. "Naomi, he took me to the roof of this magnificent building, and there, on top, several stories high, he had made a garden!"

Naomi laughed and clapped her hands. "You wouldn't have believed it if you had seen it!" Joe exclaimed.

"There were rows of wooden containers that held corn, tomatoes, zucchini, squash, beans, and all other kinds of vegetables," he said excitedly as he beamed with pride in his son. "It was amazing." Naomi smiled and closed her eyes, trying to imagine the sight.

Joe cleared his throat and sat up straighter on the swing. He pushed his feet against the porch, causing the swing to gently sway back and forth. "Naomi," he began, "at the moment I saw that garden and all those children working in it smiling and donning those proud faces, I realized something very important."

He looked forward, across the porch as he said, "Joseph is the best of me and Annie, and the best of you." Tears came to Naomi's eyes, and she lowered her head as she tried to keep her composure. She moved her hand gingerly across her lap and found Joe's hand on his hat. She softly wrapped her fingers around his hard, calloused palm.

Joe continued somewhat nervously from Naomi's soft touch. "When we lost Annie, I was lost. We were in the middle of a war, and here I was with a baby boy to look after," he said, throwing his free hand up in disbelief. "But, you ... you saved us, Naomi," he said as he squeezed her hand with gentle pressure.

He turned to look at her with softness in his eyes. "You provided Joseph with the love and compassion of a mother and provided me with the support of a wife." Unable to look upon her, he returned his gaze to across the porch. "I am so sorry you gave up your own life to save mine and Joseph's."

"Joe," Naomi responded through tears, "I lived my life just the way I wanted to, and I was honored to be a part of Joseph's life." She shook her head. "I would not have had it any other way."

She patted the back of Joe's hand with hers. Joe turned his hand over and took her hand in his, once again. Her soft and small hands felt like smooth porcelain in his large and calloused ones.

It seemed odd, but he felt fear and was nervous as he began to speak. "Naomi, at some point amid this life ...," Joe's mouth became dry, and he continued much faster than he intended, "I must confess that I fell in love with you." Naomi's face shone at the words. Joe rambled nervously, "I am sorry it has taken me so long to allow myself to share this with you, it is just that—"

Naomi interrupted with, "You are a good man, Joe, and you were a good husband. Annie was a very lucky woman."

"I do miss her, very much," said Joe as he stood up, "but I have mistaken my guilt for loyalty for a very long time. I think she is looking down from heaven, so proud of the man her son has become," he said, pacing in front of Naomi.

"I think she is also smiling over the relationship you and I have built over the years. I am nearly an old man, Naomi, and I will be losing my farm soon," Joe spoke as he moved back to his seat. Then sitting, he said, "But I know that I have everything I need right here beside me, and I am happy because of that."

Naomi reached her arms around Joe's neck and gently kissed him on the cheek. Softly she whispered in his ear, "My dear Joe, I love you too." Joe, for the first time in years, blushed.

The two sat quietly on the swing for a few minutes and said nothing. Finally, Joe mustered the courage to take Naomi's hand in his. They could not help but laugh at the odd, but pleasant feeling.

Joe placed his hat back on his head, and Naomi fixed her hair once more. Joe pushed the swing back and forth with his feet like a schoolboy on a first date. Unable to stay quiet, he said, "So, how was your day?"

Naomi laughed and shook her head at the question. "Horrible until it took a wonderful turn a few moments ago." She leaned her head on Joe's shoulder and placed his hand in both of hers. "I am no longer a teacher," she said.

Joe faced her, causing her to lift her head and meet his gaze. "I don't understand," he said.

Naomi recounted the meeting between Principal Hamilton, the Baron, and Peter's father. Joe held his hand to his mouth in disbelief. "He cares nothing about the people who work for him," Joe said. "He only cares for his bottom line."

Naomi nodded in agreement. "I will miss my classroom and watching the children grow into young adults full of hope and promise," she said with a bit of melancholy in her voice. "It is hard to believe after all the years of teaching, I still learned something new from my students every year. That's what I will miss most."

Joe was unsure of what to say. "There are other towns and other schools," he offered.

"Yes," said Naomi, "and I walked all afternoon thinking of those other towns and other schools, and those children in the other schools." She held Joe's hand tightly and stretched her shoulders. "But, I cannot help but think my time has come to fade into the background."

She leaned her head on Joe's shoulder once again. "I have always wanted to travel and learn more about other places. Will you do that with me, Joe?"

Joe smiled and kissed the top of her head. "I think I am ready for a vacation."

Chapter 22

Matt approached his parking place in front of the church and was dismayed to see it occupied by a familiar Cadillac. He parked in the next space available and gathered the box and the bagged lunch, which he had not eaten. He would have to hide the bag or risk getting an earful from Albie. Matt opened the door of his truck and slowly exited, then began to make his way to the doors of the church.

His body hurt, and his head was swimming. Every step he took felt like he was lifting anvils with his feet. He was tired, and his thoughts moved through his head as if they were Ping-Pong balls being shaken in a box.

Seeing the church, however, reminded him of Sarah, and he hoped that Albie had been successful in breaking through her shell and, perhaps, convincing her to stay. He knew if anyone could lower anybody's defenses, it would be Albie.

The decision to give Sarah the money from the donation box had not been an easy one. But the truth was that Matt believed by giving her the money, it would show their trust in her. Hopefully, the gesture would allow Albie to be more convincing in the effort to get Sarah to stay.

By receiving the means to leave, Sarah might realize her own desire to stay. There was, however, the high likelihood that Sarah would take the money and run. Then there would be very little they could do to get her to come back.

Matt tossed the brown bag into the trash receptacle outside the front doors, hopeful that Albie had not seen. Then he opened the door, apprehensive of what waited on the other side. He was immediately greeted by Duke, who ran in front of his legs and placed his hind quarters squarely against Matt's shins. Duke's tail swung back and forth, making a thud every time it hit Matt's legs. The dog raised his head and stuck out his tongue, happy to see Matt.

"That's a good boy, Duke," Matt said, kneeling down to pet his good friend. "I am very happy to see you too."

Matt took a few steps down the hall with Duke by his side. Albie was sitting at her desk, and she welcomed Matt. "Hey, Preacher. How is Mr. Paul?" Albie asked, rising from her seat.

"I would say he is okay," Matt said, "but he is very sad." He added, "They were very good together."

"That they were," said Albie. She contorted her face now, perturbed at the news she had to deliver: "You have a visitor in your office."

"Yes," Matt replied through a sigh, "I saw the car in my spot out there." He looked at Duke and asked, "You coming?" Duke quickly ran to his bed behind Albie's desk.

Albie and Matt both laughed. "Coward," they said simultaneously.

After that, Matt started back toward his office. He knew the answer, but he stopped and turned to ask the question anyway. "Sarah?" he questioned.

Albie sat in her seat and lowered her head, shaking it side to side. "She left shortly after I gave her the envelope," Albie said dejectedly. "She didn't say anything." Looking up at Matt, she added, "She just walked right out those doors."

"Thank you for trying, Albie," Matt said as warmly as he could to his friend. "I know you do not take 'no' for an answer." Albie returned a forced smile as Matt turned and made his way to his office.

"What can I do for you, Jesse?" Matt said, bursting through his office door.

"What is this, Matt?" the Baron replied. "Do we have no time for pleasantries this afternoon?"

Matt let the sarcasm in the Baron's voice go off into the void, and he responded, "What do you need, Mr. Barrister? I have quite a bit on my mind today."

"Ah, yes," said the Baron. "Millie Gentry passed away early this morning." He lowered his head and continued, "I was sorry to hear about that. She was a good woman."

Matt was surprised at the Baron's show of compassion. "Yes, she was."

"Well," the Baron continued, "I suppose that is part of the reason I am here."

Matt threw himself into one of the chairs in front of his desk while the Baron remained standing. It was not the optimum power position to be in, but Matt really did not care at this moment.

"Preacher," the Baron began in a businesslike manner, "as I mentioned to you yesterday, the numbers have been down at the factory, and we have some major shipments to get underway."

Matt picked at his fingernails and gave the Baron no indication of his recollection of the discussion. The Baron shook off the lack of response and continued, "So, I find myself in a pickle." Matt looked up; he had never heard the Baron admit he was in a hard spot before.

"You see, Preacher, I have things to get out, and we have a weekend coming, and now, we will have a funeral for a very well-liked person in our community." Now Matt saw where the Baron was headed.

"I cannot have people in and out of work like it is a revolving door." The Baron sat forcefully in the chair beside Matt. "This is what we are going to do, Preacher." He waved his hand. "Sunday's service is canceled." Then pushing his hand in a brushing motion, he said, "Have it on Saturday night, between shifts, say six o'clock." Matt shook his head in disbelief.

The Baron paid no attention to Matt's body language. "You have the Gentry woman's funeral in the afternoon on Tuesday," the Baron added. "That way we get out our shipment on Monday and can work the morning shift in its entirety on Tuesday." The Baron gave a single hard nod that indicated he was happy with his plan and that he considered the discussion over.

Matt's anger rose within him. *"Have you no shame? Have you no understanding of love or compassion?"* He stood and towered over the Baron, now wagging his finger in the other man's face. "To change the Sunday service is one thing, but to move someone's funeral because you don't find it convenient is something else!"

The Baron jumped to his feet and stepped closer to Matt. Their chests bumped slightly as the Baron countered, "You have your own opinions, Preacher, but the plans stand."

The Baron turned on his heels and made his way to the door. "See you tomorrow at six o'clock. I hope you have a motivating word for us all." Then he added in a very sarcastic tone, *"Preacher."* He moved through the door and slammed it behind him. Matt slumped back into the chair.

~~∽∾∿∾∽~~

Sarah sat on a bench on the other side of the town square from the church. Although her view of the church was obscured, she could see the cross on the steeple rising above the other buildings. She squinted as she tried to focus on the cross amid the rays of the setting sun. Her duffel bag sat on the bench beside her, and she held in her hands the envelope Albie had given her.

Sarah tried not to think about Albie, Naomi, Matt, and Joe, but she struggled to keep her thoughts from trailing back to the love and care they had each shown her. Naomi even knew her secret and had continued to show compassion toward her.

Such compassion and love had not always escaped her. For a while, her family had been the perfect picture of the all-American postcard. Her father and mother had met in high school. Neither of them came from particularly close families or belonged to any of the specific groups in their school. Separately, they were loners, but together, they were a match made in heaven.

As their time in high school came to a close, war was declared. Her father decided to enlist rather than to wait for the inevitable day his number was called by the draft board. Sarah's mother did not agree with the decision, but they both knew they did not have the connections or notoriety in the town to stave off his impending selection.

He joined the US Marines and served the bulk of the war in the Pacific. Sarah's mother felt very alone when her father left, but she was adopted by some of the families in town. They invited her to dinner and took her to church. She even took a position in the local grocery as a checkout clerk. It paid little, but it helped her pass the days.

The day the war ended, she rejoiced and was thankful her husband would be returning and they could establish their lives in the town, which she had come to call home. Her idea was not to become her reality, however.

Sarah's father returned, and he and her mother spent a blissful week enjoying the freshly declared time of peace and the prospects of a new beginning on a life that the war had put on hold. At the end of the week, her father finally told Sarah's mother news that broke her heart: he had been asked to stay on in the marines, and he agreed to reenlist.

By the time Sarah was born eight months later, the family had moved to a base several states away. Sarah's mother spent the days alone with her new baby in a house far from the life she had made for herself while her husband was away. Her mother poured all of her energy and love into her new baby and sought to give her the life she did not have, but so desperately longed for.

As was the case with most military members, Sarah's father worked long hours and left his family of two to experience most days without his presence. Sarah's mother convinced herself that this arrangement was only for a few years and then they would settle down in a quaint little town and make a life for themselves, which others could only hope for. After all, despite everything, she and Sarah's father were in love and nothing could take that away.

Over time though, the relationship became strained as loneliness and resentment grew stronger in Sarah's mother. As Sarah grew older, she was able to hear arguments through closed doors and witness her mother's frequent tears. Sarah remembered her parents' last argument as if it had happened the day before, although she was only six years old at the time.

Her father had been given orders to report to the war in Korea. The emotion of the first time he left for war flooded into her mother, and she was terrified that he would not come home. She screamed at him for moving them across the country, then abandoning them to make her a widow and his daughter an orphan.

Sarah remembered holding her stuffed bear and peeking from behind the partially closed door into her parents' room as they raised their voices at each other. Her father spied her standing there and smiled at her as he walked over and gently pulled the door closed in front of her.

He left the next day, and she never saw him again. Her mother had been correct. He died in battle in Korea, wherever that was. Her mother packed her up, along with their belongings, and they went in search of the ideal town of which her mother dreamed.

The loss of her father had left a hole in the heart of her mother that could never be replaced. Unable to bring her vision to life, her mother struggled with bouts of crying and anguish that would leave her in bed for days at a time. One fateful evening, she found solace in a drink, and it removed the edge from her emotions.

For the next several years, her mother drowned her sorrows in the bottle while Sarah tried to be the perfect child in hopes her mother would return to the woman she once was. Her mother, who had once poured every last of ounce of love she had to offer into her daughter, began to neglect her only child and to find value in the arms of men. She would stay out late and sleep through most of the morning. Sarah, at the age of ten, was taking care of herself in most regards.

The years went by, and Sarah did her best to care for her mom in the hope that her mother would one day snap out of her trance of despair. She never did, however. So, one day when Sarah was fifteen years old, she came to her mom with a plan. Her mother sat in the living room with the shades drawn, eyes staring vacantly into the open space of the sparsely appointed room. Smoke filled the room and hung in the darkness, made visible by the sunlight that found weaknesses in the shade.

Sarah had approached cautiously and fallen to her knees in front of her mother. "Let's leave here, Mama," she pleaded. "Let's start over."

The vacant stare of her mother shifted, and Sarah's mother fixed her attention on the child in front of her. She said, "You are just like your father," and then she began to yell. "He took me away and ruined my life! You ruined my life!" she shouted at a picture on the table beside her, throwing it to the ground and cracking the glass in the silver frame. Sarah jumped to her feet and stepped backward, scared. Her mother laughed at her reaction.

Sarah ran to her room and filled her father's duffel bag with what she could carry. Then she ran to her mother's room and cried as she took her mother's prized embroidered boots from her closet and placed them in the bag. As she came down the stairs, she stared at her mother who sat in the living room chair.

"You'll never make it," her mother said. Sarah quickly picked up the framed photograph from the floor where it lay in the shattered glass, and she placed it in the bag. Her mother grabbed the picture from the other side, and it froze in space as the two applied equal pressure in the opposite directions.

"You are just like him. Go on! Abandon me! Get out!" her mother screamed as she released the picture into Sarah's hands. Sarah looked at her mother, wanting to say something, but she was lost for words. She left the house and never looked back. That was two years ago.

Now, she sat on a park bench in a town in the middle of nowhere. Her mother had been right; she would never make it. The world had chewed her up and spit her out like she was a piece of used bubble gum. She felt her belly. There was no way that she could bring a child into this world, and there was no way she was fit to care for a child. She had been in her mother's way, and this child would be in hers.

Chapter 23

Matt jumped at the sound of the phone ringing on his desk. He was not sure whether he had fallen asleep or was daydreaming in his chair. Nor was he sure what time it was. It had been an arduous and long day already; now he grimaced at what news may wait for him on the other end of the phone line.

He cleared his throat and picked up the receiver. "Hello, this is Matt," he said in a weary voice.

"Wow, Preacher. You sound like you were on the losing end of a prizefighting match," Joe's voice sounded on the other end.

"You should see the other guy," Matt responded, and gave a little laugh. "You back in town or are you still in the city?"

"I'm here, over at Naomi's," Joe replied. "Listen, I heard about Millie." Joe grew a bit somber. "I'm sorry. How's Paul?"

"I suppose he is doing as well as can be expected." Matt slouched back in his chair. "How was your trip? Fruitful, I hope." Matt did not want to talk much about his day at that moment.

"It was great, Matt," Joe responded. "In fact, that's why I'm calling." He paused briefly. "How about joining me and Naomi over at the Blossom Dairy for dinner?"

"Sounds wonderful," Matt replied. "I need about forty-five minutes or so to make a phone call and a stop on the way."

"See you then," Joe said, and quickly added, "What about our friend Sarah?"

"She seems to have parted ways," Matt said with a deep sigh.

"Too bad," Joe replied.

"Too bad," Matt agreed. Both men hung up their phones.

Matt picked up the phone and immediately made a call and posed some questions to the man on the other end. Hearing what he had hoped to hear, he smiled and gave the man explicit instructions as to how he required assistance. The man was more than happy to oblige. Straightening his coat, Matt moved quickly out of his office and into the hallway.

Albie was packing up her belongings for the evening. "Preacher Matt, I guess I will be seeing you tomorrow."

"Yes … yes, you will," Matt said with a smile. "Albie, all hope may not be lost."

Albie laughed. "Now, watch out, you may start sounding like a preacher man." Matt laughed with her, and they walked out of the building together.

~∞∞∞~

Sarah had made her way to the bus station on the other side of the square. She had walked by it several times without noticing the small Greyhound symbol at the corner of the window. Apparently, it was the town post office, courthouse, and mayor's office as well. Not too many buses moved through the small Texas town, so the need for a bus station was merely an afterthought.

When she opened the glass-paned wooden door, the top of the door hit a small bell on the other side. Across the room, there was a service counter, and a funny little man popped out of a room and stood with both hands on the counter, smiling at Sarah from beneath his well-manicured, pointed moustache. Brass stands held red ropes that outlined the path between Sarah and the man. She made her way through the small maze of ropes and approached the counter.

"May, I help you?" said the funny little man, in a deeper-than-expected voice.

"I need a ticket to Mexico," replied Sarah bluntly, hoping to avoid any idle chitchat.

"Ahh, Mexico," the man said with a dreamy look in his eyes. "The Land of Enchantment." He pulled out a book and started looking through the schedules. "Well, it looks like you are in luck." He looked up from the book and at Sarah.

"Looks like we have a midnight run going to Mexico tomorrow night ... however, I do suppose that is Sunday morning, technically ... if you wanted to be formal about the whole thing."

Sarah's shoulders slumped, and she asked the man exasperatedly, "That is the only bus? What about the next bus? Where is it going?"

The man studied Sarah with a concerned look on his face. "I'm sorry, young lady, but that *is* the next bus." He chuckled. "Our little town is only a small blip on the map, so there is not much call for travel coaches to come through here."

Sarah looked at the ground and nodded, showing she understood. "Well," she said, pulling the folded envelope from her pocket, "I need one ticket on that bus."

"Fantastic," the man said, gathering materials from a cubby hidden below the counter.

He played with one of the points of his moustache. "Now, let's see here." He licked the top of a pencil and started writing on a pad of paper. "There is the international fare, the customs charge, the oversized bag charge." He paused and glanced at Sarah through the top of his eyes without moving his head up from the paper. "That big, green bag is yours, right?" Sarah nodded.

"Okay, I thought so. Sometimes you can never tell though," he said as he continued writing on his pad. "All righty," the man said, looking up from the paper and smiling at Sarah. "Looks like your trip will cost you a grand total of fifteen dollars and twenty-five cents."

Sarah's face took the news poorly. That was a good bit of money, and she had not expected a bus fare to cost so much. Nonetheless, she opened her envelope and began counting out the money. She handed the man sixteen dollars across the counter.

"Wonderful," he said as he played with the other side of his moustache. "Now, I just need to see your identification," he said as he was shuffling papers. Sarah's face went flush, partly with embarrassment and partly with anger.

"I don't have any."

"Oh no," said the man, stopping his work and looking at Sarah with a downturned mouth. "You are traveling internationally, young lady," he said. "I have to check the box here that says you have some identification."

"Please," she pleaded, "just check the box. It's no big deal." She tried to look as vulnerable as possible. "I just want to go to Mexico."

"Ah, don't look at me like that," he said. "I tell you what," he began in a chipper voice, "you tell me where you are from, and we can call and get your information from the city records." Sarah perked up. "Now, we will have to wait til Monday morning, of course," the man said, nodding and trying to get Sarah to agree.

When she did not indicate her understanding, he revealed the reason. "Town offices are closed for the weekend now I am guessing." Sarah looked at the clock on the wall behind the man. It read six thirty. She knew he was right.

"You know," the man broke the tension, "I tell you what. I would be willing to check this box if you got someone you know in town to vouch for you."

Sarah threw her head back and looked at the ceiling and sighed. She had tried to leave without saying anything to the folks who had been so kind to her. Now she was going to have to go back and ask them for help.

"Is there anybody here who can do that for you?" the man asked. "Of course, it has to be somebody I know," he added.

Sarah nodded, "Yes, I think I know of someone."

"Wonderful," the man exclaimed. "Now I am closing up for the night." Then he put his hand up to his mouth as if telling Sarah a secret. "If I don't make it home for dinner on time, the missus will put me on that bus with you." The man laughed at his own joke. "Okay, we'll see you tomorrow," he said and went back into the office.

The man reappeared out of a different door on the same side of the room as Sarah. He held out his hand in the direction of the door, indicating it was time for her to leave. She picked up her bag and walked to the door. He pulled on the handle and the bell rang. Sarah slung her duffel bag on her back and walked through the door. She was surprised to see a familiar truck parked in front of the office.

Matt smiled at her from the driver's seat. He leaned his head out of the window and called out to Sarah, "Want to go to dinner?" Nodding at the funny man in recognition, he said, "Mayor."

The man winked and nodded back. "Preacher."

Sarah turned quickly to say something, but the man swiftly moved behind the door and closed it with one more ringing of the bell. He disappeared behind a shade that had the word "Closed" written across it, and she saw his silhouette move away. She looked at Matt, and he smiled and shrugged his shoulders.

Duke jumped across Matt and stuck his head out of the window and barked once at Sarah. "C'mon," Matt said, "Naomi and Joe are waiting on us."

Realizing that Matt and the funny man had worked together to delay her departure, she shook her head and stomped her feet as she flung her duffel into the back of his truck. She walked to the other side and opened the door and sat down as hard as she could in the passenger seat. Duke leaned over and licked the side of her face. Sarah smiled thinly, and Matt laughed.

Chapter 24

Matt, Sarah, and Duke arrived at the Blossom Dairy only moments behind Joe and Naomi. Joe was just pulling Naomi's chair out for her as the two walked up. Duke took his place under the table. Joe showed a look of surprise to see Sarah standing before him, and Naomi grinned with delight as she saw the same.

Sarah said nothing as she pulled out her chair and threw herself into the seat. She had not uttered a word since Matt had picked her up at the bus station, but to be fair, he had not spoken either. Together they all took their places at the table and breathed a collective sigh as the events of a long day weighed heavily on their minds.

The three friends acted instinctively as they began their conversation without making a great deal of fuss about Sarah's presence. Naomi patted Sarah's hand from across the table, letting her know she was happy she was with them, and Joe would occasionally look her way and flash a big smile.

They did not speak about her attempt to leave without saying good-bye or her attempt at taking the money from the donation box—which she was positive they all knew by now. Her presence was welcomed, and she slowly began to feel more at ease as the conversation continued.

"You should have seen it, Matt!" Joe exclaimed with great excitement. "The tomato plants were taller than me, and big red

151

tomatoes weighed down the branches from all sides." He sat back in his chair and crossed his arms with a proud and somewhat smug look on his face. "He is just a chip off the old block." Naomi put her hand to her mouth and shook her head, trying to stifle a laugh and indicating Joe was being a bit over the top.

Joe caught her expression out of the corner of his eye and sat forward, quickly adding, "But he is great with those kids too, and well, I guess I have to say that part isn't from me."

"Sarah." Joe directed his comment at the young girl as she patted Duke's head in her lap. "I owe thanks to you for causing me to make my trip up there to see my boy."

Sarah said nothing, but looked wide-eyed at Joe and moved her finger to her chest as if to say, "Who me?"

"Yep," Joe responded, reading the question on her mind. "If you hadn't called me out on my stubbornness last night, I would have let my own pride get the best of me." Naomi and Matt looked at each other in feigned amazement.

Joe laughed. "That's right, I admitted it. I can be a bit stubborn."

Matt raised his hand and put his thumb and index finger closely together than squinted at the space through one eye. Joe threw his napkin across the table at Matt. They all laughed.

There was a brief moment of silence as Mary sat their dinners in front of them. Naomi and Joe looked in deference to Matt before they began eating, but Matt cut a piece off his country-fried steak and brought it to his mouth. Without exchanging a word or a glance, Joe and Naomi began eating as well. Sarah picked up her utensils and moved the food around her plate, and although she was very hungry, she felt very little like eating.

Matt addressed no one in particular, "I guess it is all over town by now that service is canceled Sunday and will be tomorrow night."

Naomi slammed her silverware down on either side of her plate. "Ohh, that Baron!" Her face became flushed with anger "Who does he think he is?" The more she continued, the louder she became.

"Just because he has money, he thinks he can do whatever he wants to whomever he wants! Well, I for one am tired of it!" She was on a roll and even though Joe was casually trying to calm her down by gently touching her arm as she spoke, it was not working one iota.

"He controls the factory, sure, that's his business, and it makes sense!" She conceded this point with relative ease, but then quickly moved on to say, "But to come into a school and tell a child that he cannot go to college and to fire the teacher who suggested it! Well, that is none of his concern!" Her eyes were welling up with tears as a day chock-full of emotion came to a crescendo in her heart and mind.

"I am a good teacher and my children are good students who deserve the best in life, not to be minimized by some old miser who bullies a town with his money!"

She took a deep breath, signaling she was done with her outburst. Her emotions bested her, causing Naomi to bury her head in Joe's shoulder in an effort to stifle her tears. He reached across his body and put his hand on her head.

Matt glanced at Joe and Sarah as they both were fixated on Naomi. Although she had gone through great lengths to show she was not affected by the events caused by the Baron's influence over Peter's parents and the principal, they all knew she was deeply hurt by losing her position as a teacher. She loved the students, and she loved to watch them learn. Naomi could not disguise the pain of the loss anymore and the anger she held toward the man who had taken it from her.

Matt spoke softly, "I am sorry the Baron did that to you, Naomi. He made a grave mistake and took from this town one of its best assets."

Joe added, "Everyone knows that, Naomi." She lifted her head and dried her tears on a napkin.

"What makes me most sad," she said through sniffles, "is that Peter will never know anything more than that factory because the Baron took it all from him." The two men looked on in silence, Sarah sat mesmerized by Naomi's passion, and the Blossom Dairy was quiet.

"Well, my lands, I have made a fool of myself," Naomi said. "Please give me one moment while I freshen myself up." She stood, and both men rose from their seats. "Would you care to join me, Sarah?" Naomi asked as she departed the table. Sarah startled Duke as she jumped from her seat and followed Naomi to the restroom.

As they walked away, Matt took a bite of his roll and motioned toward the ladies. "Quite a woman you got there."

Joe lowered his head and blushed. "Yes, sir," he responded. "I suppose I do."

When they reached the restroom, Naomi turned to fix her hair in the mirror. She said, "Sarah, honey, remember what we talked about this morning?" She looked at Sarah in the reflection of the mirror. "If you are going to fight off the sick feelings in your stomach, you have to eat." She turned and put her arm on Sarah's shoulder. "Now when we go back out there, you start eating, okay?"

Sarah nodded, surprised at how quickly Naomi had moved on and shifted her concern toward her. In fact, she was not entirely sure that the trip to the bathroom was for no other reason but to deliver that message.

When the two returned, the men put down their forks and stood, pulling out the seats for the ladies. Each sat and returned to eating their dinners. Sarah, feeling encouraged by Naomi, took a big bite of the cheeseburger on her plate. Joe was finished eating and proceeded to sneak leftovers under the table to Duke's waiting mouth.

"Okay, Matt," said Joe, "you have held on to that box since you got here. What's in it?"

Matt placed his hand on the box in his lap. "Ahh, it's nothing really, just a gift."

Joe leaned forward. "That is not just any gift, Matt, or it would be sitting on the seat of your truck." He moved his hand in a give-it-up motion. "Let's see it, Preacher." Matt reluctantly handed his old friend the box.

Joe pushed his chair away from the table, causing Duke's head to fall from his lap. Sensing that his food source had run dry, Duke made his way over to Matt's lap and happily received a French fry for his adjustment.

Exaggerating his anticipation as if to make a big production in opening the box, Joe lifted one end of the box and pretended to peek into the package. He could see nothing, so he removed the entire lid and handed it to Naomi. There was an envelope on top of the tissue paper, which he also removed and handed to Naomi. Naomi looked at Matt and saw that he was not smiling.

She went to stop Joe from opening the paper. "Joe, maybe ..." But it was too late. Joe unfolded the paper, and his shoulders dropped as he slumped in the chair. He looked at Matt. He looked at Naomi. Then he looked at the old leather book in the package.

"What is it?" Sarah asked, trying to see the contents of the box over the table.

Joe looked at Matt. "How? I mean, where? How did you find this, Matt?"

Matt moved his eyes back and forth between Naomi and Joe. "It came home with Billy," he said. "Millie and Paul have had it since then."

"What is it?" Sarah asked again.

Matt responded, "It is my Bible." Joe refolded the paper over the Bible and placed the envelope back in the box, then returned the lid with care.

Naomi suggested, "Rather than dessert here, why don't we go to my house for brownies and coffee." She smiled at Sarah. "I feel like baking, and Sarah can help me I am sure." Sarah returned her smile. They all agreed that the plan Naomi had proposed sounded very good.

Matt did make a small change though. "Naomi, you go ahead and start with dessert. I think I would like to walk to your house, and maybe Sarah can walk with me." Sarah's eyes widened, and after a moment of hesitation, she slowly nodded her head in agreement to walk with Matt and Duke.

"Okay," Joe jumped in, "but walk fast, 'cause I could use a brownie."

Chapter 25

The familiar sound of the bell ringing was heard as they left through the doors of the Blossom Dairy Diner. The sun was setting, and the sky glowed with a hue of orange and red that provided a comfort in the dimming light.

Matt walked toward his truck and removed Sarah's duffel from the back. He lifted the duffel and tossed it toward Joe, all in one motion. Joe was focusing on cleaning his teeth with a toothpick and nearly missed the incoming baggage. He caught it with an, "Umph," and shot Matt a pretend angry glare. Matt snickered and moved to walk with the other three to Joe's car.

"We'll catch up with ya," Matt said, opening the door for Naomi. Joe started up the car and they pulled out of the gravel lot onto the road. Matt, Sarah, and Duke made their way to the sidewalk and followed the vanishing taillights back toward town.

Sarah knew the walk was not far, but she was unsure of why Matt had made this request. The preacher had many opportunities to lecture her up to this point, and he always stopped short of doing so. She began to consider that he was going to ask for the money back or, maybe, Albie had not told him she was giving it to her or that she had tried to steal it. Even worse, she began to believe that Naomi had shared her secret, and Matt was going to tell her how evil she truly was.

But for several minutes, they simply walked in silence. With each step, the sun set deeper into the sky, and the red and orange hues were replaced with the blue and purple of the coming night.

A streetlight flickered on at the same time Matt asked, "Sarah, what is it that is missing from your life?" Sarah looked at Matt with crooked eyebrows, indicating she was unsure of what he meant by the question. "Why do you keep running?" he clarified, "and what is it that you are running from?"

The question was not one that Sarah had not considered for herself, but in an attempt to avoid answering it, she turned it back on Matt: "I don't know. What are *you* running from?"

Matt was not shocked by the question, but he leaned back with his hands in his pockets, looking at Sarah in feigned surprise as they walked. "What do you mean?" he asked, echoing her response.

She thought for a moment, then replied, "Sometimes you seem just as confused as me. I just don't get it. Every preacher I have ever met could do nothing but talk to me about the fires of hell and saving myself from my devilish ways."

She was obviously recalling some personal experiences in the not-too-distant past. "But you," she continued, "you have not mentioned anything like that once. In fact, most preachers I have met are wagging a Bible in my face, and you won't even carry one … well, except in that box you won't open." Matt glanced at the box he carried under his arm.

"So," Sarah concluded, "you can ask me what is missing or what I am running from, or whatever, but I can ask you the same thing."

Matt looked at Sarah and quietly said, "Touché."

He sighed and bent down to pick up a broken stick on the sidewalk. He threw it ahead of them, and Duke darted to pick it up. Duke found the stick, placed it in his mouth, and waited for Matt and Sarah to catch up. When they drew close, Matt took the stick from his faithful companion and threw it again.

This time, after he threw the stick, he spoke to Sarah in a quieter and more somber tone. "Sarah, I remember when I was younger, probably even younger than you, I wanted nothing more than to show the world how much God loved it."

Losing himself in the memory, he continued, "I had a constant feeling of being in the embrace of a warm and loving God. Every day I awoke to the presence of the Holy Spirit, and every night that same presence cradled me to sleep."

His eyes tried to convey happiness in his recollection, but they were overshadowed by his heartache. "I think from the moment I was old enough to know I would grow up, I knew I wanted to be a preacher."

He took the stick from Duke and threw it again. "I loved going to church, hearing the music, and seeing the Spirit of God move through the people as the service carried on." He looked at her with excitement in his eyes. "I could have done that twenty-four hours a day, seven days a week."

Matt stopped walking for a moment. "I was a good preacher too," he said. "I made house calls and hospital visits at every hour, and I never missed the chance to welcome a new family into town or a new baby into this world."

He started walking again as he continued, "I thought when the war came along, it would be my opportunity to take the gospel to the ends of the earth." He waved his free arm indicating the expanse, then he took several steps in silence. "I suppose I wasn't ready for what I would see," Matt said, barely loud enough for Sarah to hear.

"What happened?" she asked. She removed the stick from Duke's mouth and threw it ahead for him.

"War, young lady," he said looking forward with a blank face. "War is what happened." He patted the box with his hand. "The Bible in this box went with me to countless countries, and I read from it to hundreds of dying men."

Matt's eyes became glassy. "Sometimes the words brought comfort, and sometimes they did not." He shook the memories from his head. "Nonetheless, I felt strongly those words meant something, and God wanted His children to know He cared, so I read and recited the words as often as I could."

At that point, he looked at the young lady and, in her, saw the faces of the soldiers he had once offered comfort. Sarah was holding one end of the stick, and Duke walked next to her, holding on to the other end.

"Then, one day, I came across a soldier who needed to hear the words of comfort from me—" He was interrupted by a question.

"Mr. Gentry's boy, right?" Sarah asked, proud of herself for piecing together the association.

Matt nodded. "Yes, Billy Gentry." He sighed and moved his head from side to side as if to loosen the stiffness in his neck. "You see, I had seen a lot of death and violence up to that point," Matt said, "but seeing Billy on that beach … all bloodied … well, I froze."

"What do you mean?" Sarah questioned.

Without much thought, Matt responded, "With each instance of death and violence I had experienced up to that day, a little bit of me had begun to doubt my faith, and darkness seeped in."

Matt became trapped in his memories for a moment. "Everything that I believed to be true and held dear in my faith seemed to abandon me completely as I watched that boy die on the beach." Matt spoke again, nearly forgetting he was talking to a young lady. "Billy wanted nothing more than to feel at peace, but instead he felt fear."

Kneeling down, he took the stick from Duke and tossed it ahead. Returning to his walk, he said, "I lost hope and, I suppose, I threw away some of my faith. I couldn't find God in that moment. The small amount of darkness that I had allowed to seep into my heart had vanquished the presence from my childhood."

He and Sarah stopped walking. "So, thinking God had left me, I turned my back on Him. That is now my curse ... to experience the fear and despair of walking the world separated from the God who provided me with so much warmth and strength when I was young."

Sarah was unsure of what to say or how to feel about the information she had just received. Matt helped by breaking the silence. "I left this Bible on Billy's chest and have not carried one since." He shook his head at the decision, then supplied his reasoning. "I couldn't trust God, and I was sure God wanted nothing to do with me."

He went on, "I suppose it was easy to come back to a town shell-shocked by the war and in the tyrannical grips of Barrister Enterprises. People expected me to be the preacher, and I didn't know how to do anything else. Folks made little notice of the fact that I wasn't much of a minister anymore. So, I just kept up the appearance." Matt slowly returned from the spell of his past and felt chagrinned for sharing so much.

They continued to walk in silence while taking turns tossing the stick to Duke. Sarah kicked at a loose stone with her boot. "God left me alone a long time ago, so I left Him alone too." She shrugged her shoulders. "Besides, even if I wanted to go back to church, God wouldn't want me ... not now."

"I see," said Matt. "You have done things so bad that God cannot forgive you, right?"

"Yep, something like that," Sarah replied. Both of them had stopped throwing the stick, and Duke carried it in his mouth and walked beside them. Matt moved the box from under his left arm to his right, then put his hands back in his pockets.

"What do you know about the stories in the Bible?" he asked.

"Very little," Sarah admitted.

"Well, you know who Jesus is right?" Matt asked with a bit of reassurance in his voice.

"Yes, I am not stupid," Sarah replied.

"Okay, okay," Matt went on. "Do you know about the woman at the well?"

She looked at the ground, then quickly grabbed the stick from Duke and threw it. "No," she said in the middle of her throwing motion.

"This woman, an outcast woman, comes to the well to get water and finds Jesus sitting there," Matt said as he began to tell the story. "She is surprised to find Him there and even more surprised to hear Him speak to her. She is at the well in the middle of the day because she has done so many things wrong that no one else will speak to her. So, to hear someone talk to her and to later find out it is the Son of God, don't you think she was in shock?" Sarah nodded.

"Anyway," Matt continued, "she tries to hide all of her sins from Jesus, but He is able to tell them to her and call her out on them."

"Figures," Sarah asserted.

"You would think, right?" Matt responded. "But, He does that to let her know that despite what she has done, He still wants her to know that all He has to offer is available to her."

Sarah stopped walking, and Matt turned to face her. "In fact, she becomes the bearer of the good news of Christ by running to tell all of the people who wanted nothing to do with her about her encounter at the well. And do you know what, Sarah?"

Matt looked at Sarah, and she noted passion in his eyes that she had not seen before. "They all followed her back. She led them to Jesus." They both turned and began walking again. "You see, Sarah, God forgives."

Sarah was very quiet for a moment. "Yeah, but what if I don't want to forgive God?"

Matt pursed his lips and nodded his head in understanding. "I am working on that one too."

They reached the steps of Naomi's house, and Duke bounded onto the porch and laid on the mat by the door. Sarah walked up onto the first step, and Matt turned her around by gently grasping her elbow.

"Sarah," he said, standing eye to eye with her, "you and I are at a crossroads. God is telling us something by allowing us to meet and spend this time together. Both of us are lost and alone. I see myself in you, and I bet, if you look hard enough, you see yourself in me. I do not think it is a coincidence that my Bible returned soon after you came to town."

Sarah stopped him by saying, "That is silly. I had nothing—"

Matt interrupted her. "That's right. *You* had nothing to do with it. Maybe we are wrong to think God abandoned us, Sarah." He looked at her with as much compassion as he could convey.

"You are being given the chance to start a new life, Sarah. Albie will help you get on your feet, and she will help you care for your baby." Sarah nearly lost her footing as she stepped back on the stairs.

"I knew she would tell you!"

"Young lady, no one has told me a thing," said Matt. "I may be an old man, but I am not blind."

She wasn't sure whether to believe him or not, but she supposed it really didn't matter. The fact was her secret was not a secret any longer.

Matt sensed her vulnerability. "Sarah, I am asking you to stop running and to think about what brought you here. Take Albie up on her offer. She is an angel with a lot of love to give, and she will help you make a home."

Sarah walked up the remaining steps and made her way to the door. She reached down and gave Duke a few good strokes on his fur, then opened the screen door causing him to jump to his feet. Turning back, she faced Matt. "What about you, Preacher. What is your crossroad?"

Matt was not sure what to say. He knew he was asking her to place her trust in people she barely knew and to believe God had orchestrated it all and, perhaps, he was refusing to show that same trust. She looked at him as if to say, "See. That's what I thought."

Before turning to go inside, she said, "Can you please pick me up tomorrow and vouch for me at the bus station?" Matt was stung by her ability to turn cold so quickly. He said nothing, but nodded his head. Sarah opened the door and went inside, allowing the screen door to slam.

Matt's body jerked with the loud slam of the door. He had said everything right to make her consider changing her plans and staying. But his words were hollow without his own ability to hold belief in them. Sarah had perceived his weakness and used it against him. Matt scratched Duke's neck as he opened the screen door. Together, they entered the house behind Sarah.

Chapter 26

At Naomi's house, Matt only stayed long enough to enjoy the homemade brownie and half a cup of coffee. Sarah quickly finished one brownie, then wrapped another in a napkin and excused herself to her bedroom. Joe and Naomi were left alone in the kitchen to enjoy each other's company for a short time before the long day caught up with both of them as well.

Naomi walked Joe to the door. Joe, holding his hat next to his chest with his left hand and touching her arm with his right, leaned forward and kissed her cheek.

"Now I could get used to that," Naomi said with a blush. Joe made his way down the walk to his car, and Naomi was certain that she saw him skip at least once.

The night was long and restless for each of the four of them. Joe had experienced a wonderful day, and he was excited about his son's future and his own ability to finally tell Naomi how he felt about her. But he was still plagued with anxiousness over the farm, and its uncertain future.

He had convinced himself that he did not care about Joseph's decision to not take it over, but he was saddened with the thought of having the land worked by his father's family and his grandfather's family fall into the hands of a bank. He knew any land owned by the bank would soon be owned by the Baron.

Naomi also tried to come to grips with the events of her day. The blow of losing her job had been softened by the courage shown by Joe to open up his heart to her. She could not help but feel somewhat broken though. She lay in bed and watched the dancing light on her ceiling caused by the reflection of the moon off of her silver nightstand tray. The curtain would move in the gentle breeze through the small crack in the window, intermittently blocking the light through the pane.

As she studied the dancing light, she began to realize that she was sadder for Peter than she was for herself. Naomi felt she had failed him in his quest to reach for his dreams. She kept replaying the meeting in her head to think if she could have done or said anything differently to better convince the men of Peter's potential.

Her conclusion was that the problem was not the lack of understanding of Peter's potential, but it was the lack of trust and encouragement required for that potential to bloom. The Baron had made such an investment difficult for Peter's father.

Matt sat on the floor in his bedroom, and Duke stretched out across his lap. Just a few feet in front of him, the closed shirt box lay on the floor. Its once sharp edges were now bent and crumpled from Matt toting it with him all day, but it remained closed, sealing the preacher's Bible from his sight.

Duke grunted as Matt scratched his neck and ran his hand across the dog's soft brown and black fur. Duke had been his sole family member for almost ten years, and never could he have asked for a more faithful or loving dog. Duke had his full trust in Matt, and Matt was certain his friend would do anything he needed from him. He couldn't help but think that he once had that relationship with God, but he still struggled to regain the complete faith he had abandoned so long ago.

Sarah clutched the picture of her family and closed her eyes, trying to recall the love she had felt as a young child. That love had turned to hate within her and had caused her to be someone she did not want to be or to know. She looked at the baby in the picture and then sat up in the bed and looked at herself in the dresser mirror. The little girl's smile had faded, and an unhappy and hardened young woman now stared back at her.

"What am I doing?" she asked herself. Sarah placed a hand on her belly and stood. Turning, she looked at her profile in the mirror. She had not started to show yet, so she stuck out her belly. A smile briefly crossed her face, but then it quickly disappeared as she threw herself back onto her bed. She reached over and found the napkin on her night table, then opened it and removed a piece of the brownie hidden inside.

She thought of her time with Naomi and her time with Albie. They had shown her more love in two days than she had been shown in the last few years of her life put together. For the first time, she started to consider her own ability to love and wondered if it were possible for her to love her child. She was in a tight spot, and the last thing she needed was a baby to slow her down, but slowly the corners of her mouth rose into a smile as she began to envision her love for a child of her own.

~~~

Both Sarah and Naomi were up early on Saturday morning. As Sarah strolled into the kitchen, Naomi was pulling toast from the toaster and setting a cup of tea on the table for her. "I thought I heard you moving around," Naomi greeted her, "so, I thought it best to get the toaster fired up." She flashed a smile, and Sarah flashed her one in return.

Naomi filled the percolator with coffee grounds and water, then set it on the burner on the stove. Convinced everything was sealed tightly, she took a seat beside Sarah at the table. "You know, Sarah," Naomi said quietly, "you don't have to leave today."

Sarah picked at her toast and glanced at Naomi. "Oh, I know that. You all have been so kind to me, but I have to move on." Sarah averted her eyes from Naomi. "I have no choice." Naomi offered Sarah consolation through her knowing and compassionate eyes.

The coffeepot started to percolate, so Naomi stood. She moved to the stove, and as she walked behind Sarah, she leaned forward and put her arms around her, saying, "We always have choices, but we often close our eyes to the ones that are tougher to make." She patted both of Sarah's shoulders, and she straightened herself and turned to remove the pot from the burner.

Naomi had just finished pouring her cup of coffee when both she and Sarah were surprised by a knock at the door. "What in the world?" Naomi exclaimed as she rose from her seat and pulled her robe tightly closed and cinched the belt. Sarah remained seated at the table and watched Naomi as she carefully made her way from the kitchen to the living room.

As she passed the front windows, she slowed down, hoping to catch a glimpse of who her early morning visitor was. She saw nothing. As Naomi approached the door, she saw the silhouette of a man in a fedora cap through the door's curtain.

She pulled back the curtain slightly and angled her head so she could see outside without fully revealing herself to whoever stood on the other side of the door. In recognition, she opened the door and spoke through the screen, "Mr. Travis. Good morning. Is everything all right?"

Peter Travis Sr. stood on her porch and quickly removed his hat when Naomi opened the door. "Yes, ma'am—well, no ma'am, everything is not okay," Mr. Travis said. Just then, Naomi saw Peter standing to the edge of the porch, just out of view.

"Ms. Rhodes," he continued, "I cannot say that I am happy with the events of yesterday or proud of my inability to challenge some of the thoughts in the room." Naomi began to offer a word of consolation, but Mr. Travis held up his hand and asked for just a moment to speak. Naomi nodded in acquiescence.

"I am sure you understand the pressure I was under from certain parties." Mr. Travis tried to keep eye contact with Naomi, but his embarrassment caused him to glance often at the hat in his hands.

"Mr. Barrister is a demanding person to work for and can be pretty ornery if he does not get his way. But he has shown a keen interest in my boy over the last year or two." He looked at Peter and smiled. "Peter is a hard worker with a good head on his shoulders, and that gets noticed around the factory. It is something that makes me very proud, Ms. Rhodes."

"I understand," replied Naomi, but offered no more, sensing Mr. Travis was leading up to something.

"You see, it wasn't until after our meeting yesterday that I realized that Mr. Barrister didn't care about Peter or me or our family." Mr. Travis looked at Naomi with an expression of anger combined with sadness. "All he cares about is bringing in the most money he can for himself, and well, my boy helps him do that."

He shuffled his feet a bit and continued, "No one from my family has ever gone to college, Ms. Rhodes. We have done factory work for generations. We have moved around to find jobs, and we work hard when we get them. Working at the Barrister plant is tough, but it is a good paycheck for good work." He lowered his tone, "I suppose I was clouded by what I knew, without taking time to listen to what could be."

He motioned for Peter to join him. Peter came over and stood beside his father and timidly greeted Naomi, "Good morning, Ms. Rhodes."

"Good morning, Peter," she said and smiled.

"My son has something he would like to tell you," Mr. Travis said and nodded in encouragement to his son.

"I will be attending the university this fall, Ms. Rhodes," Peter said with great excitement. Naomi hurriedly opened the screen door and hugged the young man. Mr. Travis stood back and laughed as the two celebrated.

Naomi stepped back and made sure her robe was presentable. "That is wonderful news. Just wonderful!"

Mr. Travis held out his hand, and Naomi grasped it in a firm handshake. "Thank you for pushing Peter and helping him earn this opportunity," he said.

"You are very welcome," Naomi replied.

Then losing his smile, Mr. Travis added, "I am sorry you lost your job."

The apology meant a great deal to Naomi, but she downplayed her emotions. She said in a reassuring voice, "It was probably time to move on."

Peter's father put his arm around the shoulder of his son and led him down the steps from the porch. They both turned and faced Naomi. "I'm sorry for the early morning visit, but I have to get to work," Mr. Travis said as he placed his fedora back on his head.

"I understand," said Naomi. As the father and son turned to go, Naomi called after Mr. Travis, "What pushed you to change your mind?"

He turned with a coy look. "You and Mrs. Travis are both smart ladies." The two men turned and moved down Naomi's walk toward their car. Naomi's heart was filled with joy, and she waved as they pulled away from the curb.

Chapter 27

Naomi nearly floated around the house for the rest of the morning. After coming inside from her impromptu meeting with Peter and his father, she had been singing or humming a tune consistently. She had even tried to cajole Sarah into dancing with her a couple of times, and although Sarah laughed, she never was convinced to move her feet.

She would take Naomi's hands as Naomi swayed back and forth, then Sarah would quickly sit down again. Naomi would laugh and continue her melodies as she moved through the house. She was truly happy, and she could not hide that fact.

Sarah eventually made her way to the bedroom and began to prepare herself for the day. She laid out a sundress she had chosen while in the clothes closet at the church. The fabric was a blue-and-white pattern accented by yellow daisies over the entire dress. It reminded Sarah of the dresses her mother wore when Sarah was young. Plus, it was sure to be comfortable on the long bus ride she had to look forward to. She pulled her family photograph from the bag and studied it one last time before quickly shoving it back in between layers of clothes.

She brushed her hair in the mirror and laughed when she heard Naomi singing out of key in the living room. She had to admit it was a great feeling to be in a place that felt like a real home should. Sarah paused as she moved the brush through her hair and looked at herself in the mirror. Then she went back to the bag and pulled out the photograph of her family once again.

Setting the brush on the dresser, she took a step back. Then she held the picture in front of her with her left hand and clasped her hair in her right hand, holding it above her head. She glanced at the picture and then at the mirror. At first she was amazed, but then she began to cry. She looked exactly like her mother. In her quest to become something different, she had transformed into exactly what she was running from.

Sarah placed the picture facedown on the dresser and studied herself in the mirror. "I am not her," she told herself. "I am different. I am stronger." She picked up the brush and pulled it through her hair. Looking in the mirror, she lowered her eyes. She was not sure that she was different or stronger.

Naomi knocked on the door. Sarah wiped her eyes with her palms and indicated to Naomi that it was okay to come in. She entered the room with a concerned look on her face. "Are you okay? I thought I heard you crying." Sarah said nothing, but the redness around her eyes and the blotches on her face gave her away.

Naomi did not make any mention of these clues but went straight toward the sundress on the bed. "Oh, Sarah, this is a beautiful dress." Sarah was thankful for the redirection.

"Yes it is. It was in the closet at the church."

"Well," Naomi exclaimed, "if you are going to wear this dress, then you must let me do your hair." The sadness of Sarah's face gave way to a thin smile, and she nodded.

Naomi stood behind Sarah and looked in the mirror. Reaching for the brush, she noticed the silver frame on the dresser. She lifted the frame by the corner and revealed the young parents with the baby on the mother's knee. "What a beautiful family," Naomi remarked.

Sarah was unsure of what to say. She wanted to pretend the picture was not there, so she tried to ignore the comment. Naomi, sensing this photo to be the cause of the turmoil, laid it back on the dresser. "I can see where you get your beauty from," Naomi said, pulling Sarah's hair back. "Your mother is a beautiful woman."

"Was," whispered Sarah.

"I'm sorry," said Naomi, "I didn't know she was—"

"She isn't," interrupted Sarah. "She just isn't beautiful anymore." Naomi separated Sarah's hair into three sections and began to fashion them into a French braid. "We are going to miss you around here, young lady," Naomi said, trying to pay attention to the braid.

Sarah said nothing, but turned quickly and wrapped her arms around Naomi's waist and laid her head on Naomi's chest. She began to cry hard. Naomi wrapped her arms around the young girl and let her release all of the hurt and sadness that was bottled up in her small frame. "Won't you stay?" asked Naomi.

A short time later, Matt pulled up in front of Naomi's house. He looked at his watch. He was later than he had planned, but he had delayed his arrival in order to give Sarah time to change her mind. In order to keep his word, however, he had to get Sarah to the bus station before it closed so she could her ticket to Mexico.

He was hopeful she no longer wished to go. They were not on the porch waiting for him, so perhaps that was a good sign. He opened his door and his shoes hit the street, followed by Duke's paws. Duke bounded up to the porch and laid down on the mat under the swing. Matt knocked on the door lightly.

After a few moments the door opened, and through the screen door Matt saw Sarah in a beautiful sundress with her hair pulled back in a braid. She glanced at him through the door. "Well, good afternoon," he said.

Duke jumped up and ran to the door to get in on the greetings. Sarah pushed open the screen door and in the same motion, reached for her duffel bag that was just inside. She moved the bag out to the porch and put her jean jacket on over her dress.

Matt's heart sank a bit in his chest. "Going somewhere?" he asked.

"Mexico," she replied matter of factly. "The plan has always been Mexico."

Naomi opened the screen door and stepped onto the porch. Duke immediately rolled on his back and wagged his tail rapidly. Naomi was amused by the dog's antics and reached down and gave him a good scratch on his belly. She stood and looked at Matt, then at Sarah, then back at Matt. Then she shrugged her shoulders as if to say, "I cannot make her do what she does not want to do."

Matt smiled in consolation and picked up Sarah's green duffel bag and walked down the steps back to the truck. He slung the bag into the back of the truck, opened the door, and whistled for Duke. Duke came bounding down the steps and jumped into the truck. Sarah started to move down the steps, but stopped and turned back toward Naomi and gave her a long hug. Naomi returned the embrace.

As the two let go of each other, Naomi said, "You are loved, Sarah. You may not think it, but you are loved." Sarah fought back tears as she turned and quickly made her way to the truck.

Matt shut the passenger side door and waved to Naomi. "I will see you later at the church." Naomi waved and nodded in agreement.

Sarah's heart felt heavy as they drove away from the comfort of Naomi's home. Her resolve was set strong though, and she was determined that the answer to her most immediate problem was in Mexico. Duke laid his head on Sarah's lap, and she could not help but run her fingers through his fur and play with his soft ears.

She looked forward and tried not to think about the possibility of staying in this small Texas town and starting anew. She was damaged and no one, despite what they said, could truly love her or accept her knowing all the mistakes she had made.

As she was looking out the truck's windshield, she noticed on the dashboard, in front of Matt, the familiar shirt box. It struck her as odd that Matt, since receiving the box, refused to open it and reveal its contents, but carried it everywhere with him. Knowing what the box contained made it seem even stranger.

She thought of his conversation with her on the walk to Naomi's house the night before. Matt had told her wonderful things about forgiveness and acceptance, but when asked, had to admit that he struggled with finding the faith and trust in his own heart to accept those things. Sarah thought to herself, *If he can't do it, then I definitely can't do it.*

Matt looked out over the shirt box and through the window as they drove through town. He sought the right words to say, but struggled. He had put most of his cards on the table the night before, and it had very little effect on the young girl. She was strong and stubborn—both good traits when used for a good cause. But, in this case, the attributes worked against her as she refused the love and support of people truly seeking to help her.

She had been hurt badly and had relied on herself for so long that she did not know how to trust or to have faith in others. Matt tried to think of the right words to influence her, but sadly, came up empty.

As they approached the familiar building with the small Greyhound symbol on the window, Sarah noticed a smiling face sitting on the bench in front of the entrance to the town hall. "Albie?" she questioned. Matt nodded in the affirmative and pulled his truck to the curb.

Albie stood from her bench. She was dressed in a beautiful purple-and-pink floral print dress and wore a purple pillbox hat with pink ribbon wrapped around it. In one hand, she held a canvas bag, and with the other, she waved at Sarah.

Sarah stepped out of the truck and onto the sidewalk. Albie walked up to her and grabbed the girl in a bear hug and held on tightly for what seemed like an eternity to Sarah. She did not mind though, and even laughed a little bit at the joy the embrace ignited within her. Albie released her grip and stepped back from Sarah, but kept her hands on the girl's shoulders.

"My girl Sarah," Albie said, "I sure did hope you would stay." Sarah looked down at the ground and gave a slight nod indicating she knew that was true. Matt opened the driver's side door and made his way to the back of the truck and grabbed Sarah's duffel bag from the bed.

Albie reached into the canvas bag and pulled out a piece of paper and showed it to Sarah. "This is my address and the phone number at the church." She squinted a bit as she pointed her finger at Sarah. "If you ever need a place to call home, it is right here on this piece of paper. So, don't you lose it."

Sarah, holding back tears, softly said, "Okay." Albie placed the paper back in the bag and grabbed both handles, then pulled the opening apart. She showed the contents of the bag to Sarah, who laughed through her sniffles.

"I figured the way you worked through these the other morning, you might need a couple of sleeves," Albie said, pointing at several sleeves of crackers in the bag. "But I also made you some sandwiches, and there is some fruit in there too." She closed the bag and put the handles in a single hand and held it out for Sarah to grasp.

Sarah accepted the bag and as she did Albie closed her arms around her in another embrace. This time, the embrace was softer and shorter. Albie pulled away, and tears formed in her eyes. She cupped Sarah's face in her hand and showered her with all the love a single expression could supply. Sarah fought her own tears and closed her eyes.

Albie moved to the truck, and Matt opened the door for her. She sat in the passenger seat beside Duke and fixed her eyes forward. Matt closed the door for her and walked to Sarah. He put his arm around her and led her to the door of the town hall with the duffel bag slung over his back.

The door was locked, but when they rang the bell, the funny little mustached-man appeared and let them in. "Mayor," Matt greeted him with a nod.

"Preacher," the man returned the greeting. Then he looked at Sarah and opened his arms. "Ahh, my young traveler, off to Meh-he-co." He quickly made his way around the counter and pulled out a booklet of papers and a stamp, which he vigorously started applying to the papers.

"Now this bus, if you remember, does not leave until midnight," the man said without looking up from his paperwork. He was now scribbling something in the images made by the stamp.

"Preacher," the man said, placing the booklet on the counter's second tier, "I need you to initial here, here, and here, then sign there."

Matt turned his head from the booklet to Sarah and asked, "What happens if I don't?"

"Well," said the mayor, "she won't be able to travel. You are vouching that she is who she says she is." Matt considered this for a moment. In fact, he had considered this all night. He had the power to delay Sarah's trip even longer, allowing them more time to convince her to stay. But, what good would it do? It might serve to strengthen her resolve to leave. The choice had to be hers, and unfortunately, he knew that was the only way.

Sarah swallowed hard as she noticed Matt's delay in offering his signature. Just as she was about to urge him to sign, the scratch of the pen could be heard on the paper as Matt signed the document.

Matt pushed the booklet back to the mayor. "Little lady, that will be fifteen dollars and twenty-five cents," the mayor announced as he pushed his wire-rimmed glasses up on his nose and looked over the counter at Sarah.

She pulled the folded envelope from her jacket pocket and retrieved the money to pay for the ticket. She was careful to avert her eyes from Matt as she exchanged the money, because she knew he had hoped it would be used for other things. The mayor put one final stamp that read, "PAID," on the ticket booklet and handed it to Sarah.

"The bus will probably pull in around ten o'clock and be ready to board about eleven thirty," he instructed Sarah. She nodded. "Have a safe trip," he said, then nodded at Matt and disappeared into the back room.

"Eleven thirty is a long time from now." Matt offered to Sarah, "Why don't you hang with me until then. We can go to church and then dinner before your trip."

Sarah told him that she appreciated the offer but thought it best to stay put. "I think I will just wait here," she said and noticed the disappointment in Matt's face. She was not really sure what to say to Matt, and he was not entirely sure what to say to her.

They stood in silence for a moment until he broke it by saying, "You have the number for the church. You call it if you need me or Albie." Sarah nodded.

"Thank you," she said. "Not just for the number, but for everything."

Matt shrugged. "I wish I could have offered you more." He held out his hand to shake Sarah's, but she reached past his hand and put her arms around him in a quick embrace. He put his arms around her and patted her back.

She released him and stood back, leaning to pick up her duffel bag. "Please tell Joe good-bye for me," she said, standing back up with her bag.

"I will," Matt said with a forced smile.

She turned and made her way to a bench against the wall as Matt made his way to the door. He stopped before exiting and turned to wave. Her head was in her hands, and she did not see him as he pushed the door open and went outside.

Chapter 28

Matt walked slowly to his truck, pausing a few times to contemplate returning inside to convince Sarah to come with him and to stay with Albie. Each time, he was unable to convince himself to turn around. If he was not able to convince himself, then surely he would not be able to convince Sarah.

He knocked on the hood of the truck as he passed in front of it, and Albie gave him a solemn smile. He opened his door and pulled himself into his seat. Albie and Duke both turned their heads to him as if they were waiting for him to say something, but he just sighed deeply and turned the key in the ignition of the truck. Without looking at Albie, he reached over Duke and patted her hand with his. Then he put the truck in gear and drove away.

The duo drove to the church where Matt still needed to outline his sermon. Albie would take care of readying the church for the service, which was always a huge help. But, the Baron had really applied the pressure when he changed the service to Saturday night. Matt's thoughts hung on the Baron's power as he pulled into his parking space in front of the church.

Albie had changed the sign in front of the church to read, "It's the Saturday Night Special, 6:00 p.m., Bread of Life—All You Can Eat." Matt glanced over at Albie who put her head down and snickered. "Sometimes I think you like making my life difficult," he quipped.

"No, Preacher," she countered, "I just keep you on your toes."

They entered the church, and Matt went straight to his office. Albie went into the chapel where she started setting out hymnals and tidying up from the Wednesday night activities. Duke followed Matt back to his office and immediately found his bed when Matt opened the door. Before Matt sat at his desk, Duke was snoring.

Matt could not help but laugh. "Ain't that the life." He shook his head and set the shirt box on his desk. Then he opened the top drawer and removed a pen and paper and set them in front of him. He closed his eyes and put his fingertips to his temples as he leaned forward on his elbows. As he tried to focus, his thoughts became clouded by past memories and present anxiety. He moved his fingertips in circles against his head, hoping to ease the stress and ward off the oncoming headache.

He repeated the Bible verse to himself over and over again, getting slower and more deliberate with each recital. He had given so many sermons on the verse that it seemed almost meaningless to him as he said it aloud for the fourth time: "And whatsoever ye do, do it heartily, as to the Lord, and not unto men; Knowing that of the Lord ye shall receive the reward of the inheritance: for ye serve the Lord Christ."

The Baron's belief was that Colossians 3:23–24 gave him the right to drive his work force, and they were commanded by none other than God Himself to work for him mightily and unselfishly. He seemed to skip over the idea that the Lord was above men— including *him*.

Matt continued to repeat the verse in an effort to find his voice. But as he recited the words, they took shape in his mind's eye of past events. He saw Billy lying in the sand as he walked away. His boots left prints that briefly filled with water at each step. The smoke from the battle remained heavy in the air, and it gave an appearance of clouds and darkness in the middle of the day.

The Bible sat on Billy's chest with the young man's hand holding it in place over his heart. He imagined Millie holding the Bible the same way as she lay in her bed, fighting disease and a broken heart. In holding the Bible to her chest, she had felt close to her son. For years, she had read its words and found hope in reuniting with her boy. Paul provided him testimony that her hope had been realized.

Then he thought of Sarah. He envisioned her as she sat in the town hall on a dark bench next to a bare wall. She held her head in her hands, and her face was obscured from his mental picture. In his mind, he walked to the door and turned to wave, but this time Sarah looked up. "Why don't you carry a Bible?" she asked, then buried her face in her hands once again.

Matt woke from his self-induced trance with a start. Duke rolled in his dog bed and positioned himself on his back throwing all four legs into the air. Matt looked around the room and pulled his hands back over his face while taking a deep breath in.

As he took in the breath, he felt something he had not allowed himself to feel for a very long time. It was as if an old familiar friend had reached out and touched him on the shoulder. His body leapt with excitement, happiness, fear, and awe all at the same time. There was no one else in the room, but he did not feel alone.

The presence of his youth enveloped him, and his chains of anxiety and panic, which had held him hostage for so long, became weak and fell away. For the first time since he knelt beside Billy on the beach all those years ago, Matt was free from his own captivity, and he fell to his knees in prayer.

He felt guarded at first and seemed lost for words as he struggled to convey his thoughts, but he focused on the Lord's

Prayer, which led him to his own words and conversation with God. As his thoughts formed into words, he felt anger arise in him

"You abandoned me, God. You abandoned Billy. You abandoned countless soldiers on a countless number of days! *Why did You abandon us?*" He proclaimed his words aloud and with passion, "We served You, and You left us. You let Billy and so many others die, but me—You have allowed me to wallow in doubt."

He stood beside his desk and slammed his fist down hard, causing Duke to quickly turn over and jump to his feet. *"Don't you understand I need You, Lord? Don't You understand I am lost without You to lead me?"*

His fist landed beside his letter opener, and the impact had caused the letter opener to move in the air and flip onto his hand. Weak, he leaned on his desk and opened his eyes briefly to see what he had moved, and he spied the tool next to his hand. He quickly grasped the opener and held the cold metal in his hand. He was transported to his conversation with the Baron just a few days earlier where the Baron had used the tool to define his thoughts on perspective.

That conversation now came rushing back to Matt, and he slumped in his chair and placed his head on his forearms as they rested on his desk. His hands still clasped in prayer, Matt formed the words that had eluded him for far too long: "My God, You did not abandon me. I abandoned You." The epiphany greatly distressed Matt and, again, he fell to his knees. "Father, forgive me! Father, please forgive me."

He sat in silence with his head bowed for several minutes. Tears flowed from his eyes as the pain of his seclusion and the despair of his broken heart was mended by the Holy Spirit's hands. If asked, he would not have been able to describe the thoughts or feelings that went through his mind and body during that time. But when he lifted his head and opened his eyes, it was his perspective that had changed.

He reached for the box in front of him, took the lid off, and threw it across the room. Duke followed the box top as it hit the wall on the other side. Carefully Matt lifted the old Bible from the box and placed it in front of him. His hand moved slowly over the weathered leather cover. The edges were tattered, and the leather was torn in places. He placed his thumb in the center of the book and turned back the pages, knowing exactly where the Bible would open.

Just as expected, the Bible opened to Psalm 27 as if by memory. Matt studied the page for a moment. Billy's handprint was prominent in the middle of the page. The stain had turned a brown and copper color over the years, but when Matt saw the stain, he envisioned the bright red blood that had covered the page on the day the print was made. The print was smeared as a result of the exchange between Matt and Billy, but it was visible enough that Matt could place his hand in its outline.

He moved his finger through the Scripture and found the words he had read to Billy to help him calm down and face an impending death. Billy wanted to see God and to feel God, but his fear and his pain had clouded God from his vision. Matt thought the answer was to read him the psalm where King David felt the same way. Unfortunately, he had not had time to finish, and the effect had dire consequences for the young soldier and for Matt. In striving to see and to find God, they had both lost sight of God.

Matt read the psalm aloud, and his voice became stronger as he read the words. Duke's ears twitched with each inflection, and he angled his head inquisitively with each emphasis of punctuation. The preacher in Matt was bubbling to the surface, and by the time he reached the last verse, he was standing on his chair and raising his hands in praise. The prodigal preacher returned to God.

Chapter 29

Joe arrived just in time to collect Naomi before heading to the church service. "Where on earth have you been, Joe?" asked Naomi as she hurriedly made her way down the walk and sat in the front seat of his car.

"I got held up at the bank," he said as he shut her door and ran around the front of his car.

"You got robbed?" Naomi asked, with an expression of shock. "Are you okay?"

"No, I did not get robbed," Joe said with a laugh. "I got held up … delayed."

"I knew what you meant," said Naomi. "I just thought I'd play along for you." Joe put the big Buick into gear and drove to the church.

His morning had been quite a tumultuous one, and he had not planned on it taking up the considerable part of the day it did, but the outcome of his time was very promising. The night had been incredibly draining for Joe as he considered the option for his property and his inability to manage it properly by himself. Even if he was able to bring in the crop this season, there would always be the worry of managing the next.

He had called Mr. Kelly at the bank early in the morning and had asked to meet. Luckily, Mr. Kelly himself had picked up the phone, and the two decided to meet that morning.

"What happened at the bank?" asked Naomi, taking one look at her hair in the rearview mirror.

"I suppose it's something we can talk about when there is more time," Joe responded, "but, to put it simply, I sold the farm." Naomi's jaw dropped as she turned and looked at Joe with astonishment.

"I wanted to still get something out of it," Joe said in response to the look he had received. "I needed to get something out of it to give to Joseph."

Naomi sat back in her seat and grasped Joe's right hand in hers. "Why, now?" she asked.

"Joseph does not need the distraction, and I cannot do it anymore." He adjusted himself in the seat. "My body is sore, and I am getting old. Naomi, I was going to start going into debt, and it would be for nothing."

He glanced at Naomi and flashed a smile. "You know what was funny? I drove back from Austin yesterday and thought about how excited I was for Joseph and how upset I was with myself for not opening my eyes sooner. But it was in that reflection that I realized that maybe it was time for me to reexamine my life."

She smiled as he continued, "A lot changed yesterday and, for the first time in a long time, I feel content."

Joe did not bore Naomi with details, but his effort to work out a deal with the farm was not just to protect Joseph from debt or to allow him to retire. The deal he brokered with Mr. Kelly put the property in the domain of the bank under a trust that stipulated the property could be used for no other reason than farming for fifty years.

The bank would rent the property to larger enterprises, and the collection of the rent combined with a portion of the sales would be enough for the bank to draw a gain on the investment. Joe would receive an allotment from the trust, which would be extended to Joseph upon his passing. The trust could be restructured in fifty years to no longer include a member of Joe's family.

Joe knew the trust allotment would not amount to much, but it was something for him to retire on and to help keep Joseph on his feet in times of need. He felt he was doing what he could to preserve his work and protect any development of the property by the Baron.

In an effort to change the topic, Joe asked Naomi, "What about Sarah? Did she stay?"

Naomi's face became solemn, and she shook her head. "Matt took her to the station earlier this afternoon."

Joe pulled into a parking space across the street from the church. Naomi went on, "If we would have had more time … I think she might of … well, maybe she would have stayed."

Joe patted her hand. "We can't make people do things; we can only help them see what it might be like if they choose differently."

Naomi nodded in agreement. "You never know, maybe Matt and Albie had some luck at the station." She paused, "But I am not holding my breath. I think we would have heard."

Joe opened his door, left his seat, walked around the car, and opened Naomi's door for her. He held out his hand, which she took, and pulled herself from her seat. The two walked hand in hand across the street and into the white double doors of the church.

Sarah sat on the hard bench outside of the town hall. The funny little mustached man had asked her to wait outside as he locked the doors to the building. He apologized profusely, but said it would not be proper to leave a person in the town hall unattended.

She wondered if by "person" he was referring to only her, or whether he would perform the same actions with all people. Nonetheless, she found herself on a wooden bench all alone in the center of a town that was likely not on a single map.

Sarah felt small. Her stomach growled, and the unpleasant sound was followed by a sharp pang right below her ribs. She had not eaten since breakfast, and it was very much to her stomach's dislike.

She opened up the bag Albie had given her, and among other things found a container of jam and a sleeve of crackers. She removed the jar and unscrewed the top, then using her nail, popped the airtight top from the glass mouth. The smells of strawberries and sugar quickly wafted to her nose and caused her stomach to growl again in anticipation. She was salivating as she hurriedly reached into the bag to remove one of the sleeves of crackers. In her haste, her hand also grabbed the information Albie had given her.

She set the sleeve beside her and grasped the note in one hand, unfolding it. The message was short and sweet: "My girl Sarah, you are always welcome to call this place home." Below the message was the contact information Albie had promised. Part of Sarah wanted to call the number or run to the church right then and there. But it meant choosing a harder life. It meant facing stares and hearing ridicule from those who purported to be so much better than she. It meant the responsibility of a child and the need to love and care for that child, forever.

Sarah was making the right decision. It was easy. Nothing would change. She could come back from Mexico and start over, she thought. Maybe she would go to the East Coast this time. She was certain there were opportunities for her there.

She sat on the bench daydreaming about a perfect life in New York City as she imagined it to be. Maybe she would meet someone famous, and maybe she would live happily ever after in a mansion with a man who adored her. "After all, isn't that the fairy tale for every young girl?" she asked herself.

Her stomach growled again, and she reached down beside her and found the sleeve of crackers. Tearing open the sleeve on one end, she retrieved a cracker and dipped it in the strawberry preserves. The sweet jam blended perfectly with the salt from crackers, and she closed her eyes as she tasted such harmony.

Sarah opened her eyes and fixed her gaze to the edge of the town square where she could see the white steeple of the church rising above the other buildings. She squinted to protect her eyes from the setting sun, and she listened carefully as she heard the church bell began to ring.

Chapter 30

Albie pulled down on the rope one last time, and the bell, high above her head, pulled to one side, allowing the hammer to strike the side of the bell that rang the last call to worship. She wrapped the rope around a metal latch and entered the sanctuary. When she found her seat in the rear of the large room, she sat down unceremoniously.

Typically, Duke was waiting for her when she sat, but this time, he was not there. She began to worry. She had not seen Matt emerge from his office, and when she had knocked on his door to bring him food earlier, he did not open the door and politely declined the offerings. By this time, however, he was usually sitting near the pulpit and ready to get started. He always said, "The earlier we start, the earlier we finish."

Naomi and Joe had also made notice of Matt's absence. They looked across the pew at Albie, who threw her hands up and shrugged, indicating she was aware he was missing but unsure of the preacher's location as well. Joe looked at his watch, than looked worriedly at Naomi. The doors to the front of the church opened, and the people in the church turned in unison.

The Baron strode into the church, grabbing either side of his blazer, and his wife held on to his elbow; both were nodding and smiling as they made their way down the aisle. Joe turned his head toward Naomi and rolled his eyes. The Baron's wife sat in the front pew, then nodded to everyone; the Baron sat beside her and cleared his throat. There was still no preacher, and the room fell silent.

A minute or two went by, but to Naomi, Joe, and Albie, it felt like an hour or possibly more. Joe, unable to withstand the pressure of not knowing where his friend was, leaned toward Naomi and whispered, "I am going to get him." Naomi nodded her approval.

Before Joe stood, however, the side door to the sanctuary opened, and Duke ran into the room, quickly moving to the back and laying on the floor beside Albie. "Good dog," Albie said, scratching Duke's head.

Most eyes had followed Duke along his path, and everyone was surprised when they heard the door close and turned to see Matt in a stole and vestments. He had not worn anything of the sort for as long as most people remembered.

Matt's eyes locked with Joe's, then Naomi's, then Albie's. He gave a small nod to each, exuding a passion and confidence long missing from his eyes. Then his eyes locked with the Baron's.

Jesse Barrister had never seen such a look from the preacher and was taken aback by its intensity and determination. Matt made his way to the pulpit and did not unlock his gaze on the Baron until he reached the steps and needed to make sure of his footing.

Rising in front of the congregation, he turned and addressed them in a voice with which they were unfamiliar and in a tone that was surprisingly rich and vibrant. "Tonight, I have been asked to speak to you from Colossians 3:23–24, which says, 'And whatsoever ye do, do it heartily, as to the Lord, and not unto men; Knowing that of the Lord ye shall receive the reward of the inheritance: for ye serve the Lord Christ.'" The Baron smiled, and Matt could hear the collective sigh of the others in the room. No matter how he was dressed or how he changed his delivery, they had heard this before.

Matt held out his hands to assuage any probable comments that might be brewing in the members of his congregation. "I am going to do things differently tonight, since this is a special Saturday-night service." He looked hard at the Baron. "Let's skip some things and just jump right into the sermon." He looked over apologetically at Mrs. Carlton on the piano.

The congregation started looking around at one another in discomfort, and a collective mumbling could be heard. The Baron started laughing. His laughter began to drown out the whispers until all was quiet except his baritone laugh. Joe held Naomi's hand and watched his friend with anticipation.

Without taking his eyes off Matt, Joe leaned his head to the side and whispered, "He's back."

Naomi glanced at Joe, then at Matt; immediately she saw what Joe saw. Matt's eyes were closed, and his mouth was moving in prayer. As they watched, Matt clasped his hands then raised them up in the air while opening his eyes. "Peace be with all of you," he exclaimed. The Baron's laughter stopped, and the congregation responded, "And with you."

"We should do all work as if we work for the Lord, right?" Matt began. "Isn't that what you want me to say, Mr. Barrister?" He glanced down at the Baron and shrugged inquisitively. The Baron's eyes turned cold and the smile left his face.

"Unfortunately, that passage was written to describe the relationship between master and slave, a sad reality of the times in which Paul lived. Well, I am here to tell you that you all are the hardest working and most dedicated people to the job that I know, but you are by no means slaves."

The murmurs began again and stopped quickly as Matt continued, "I have told you so many times to work harder because that is what God is asking of you, but I was wrong. That is what your employer was asking of you."

The Baron stood up, but before he could say anything, Matt continued, "God does not care how many pieces or parts you put out in an hour. That does not concern His bottom line."

"Now you wait a minute. I will not have you—" the Baron interrupted Matt's sermon.

"Sit down and be quiet, or leave," Matt responded without allowing the Baron to finish. The Baron looked at the faces in the room. He was not used to being spoken to in such a manner, and people were not used to hearing him spoken to like that.

His face became red with anger, and he began to say something, but his wife stood and whispered something in his ear, while she looked around the room uneasily. In response to her comment, he slowly took his seat but refused to remove his stare from the man who stood a few short feet in front of him.

"The passage in Colossians does not mean that we are required to be a slave to our jobs or our employers. The passage means that we should work in our daily lives, knowing that our true reward is in the salvation we have received from Jesus Christ." Matt's face beamed with excitement. Then he exhibited a more stoic presence. "But I forgot that."

He stepped down and began to walk through the aisle. "I took my eyes off God, and because of that I have failed you as your pastor and your shepherd." He spun on his heels and moved back toward the front of the church.

"By working for the Lord, we are keeping our focus on God and leading our lives in a way that delights God. But when we let our eyes fall, and we no longer look to God but to ourselves for answers, we become lost. We misplace priorities and look for worth in our own minds and the words of others. When we don't find what we are looking for, we feel alone. We feel abandoned."

Matt jumped over the steps and made his way behind the pulpit. He placed his hands on the side of the pulpit and stated emphatically, "We must have faith in God and trust in His eternal presence.

"However," he continued, "faith can be tested in the world in which we live. It is easy for us and those around us to take our eyes and our focus off God." He had the congregation's attention, and they hung on each word he said.

"Most of us have lived through the times of war, and have unfortunately been touched by the hands of destruction and death as a result." Men and woman turned to each other and nodded knowingly in remembrance of those dark times. Matt stepped out from behind the pulpit, feeling it put a barrier between him and the people with whom he was speaking.

"On the middle of a beach on the day many people remember as the war's greatest day, I experienced my darkest hour." He found Paul Gentry in the congregation, and the two men acknowledged each other briefly. Matt knew this was going to be hard, but he already knew Paul understood. His palms became moist with perspiration, but he paid little attention to his body's standard reaction to the memory.

"I knelt with a dying young man and looked for God. God had become harder for me to find in the midst of chaos and darkness. This time, I chose to not find God. I blinded myself from God by seeing the pain, the misery, the loss, and the chaos that were all present in a world separated from God. I was broken, and I was lost. I believed this was a world in which God was not present."

He fought the mental return to the time at the beach and from becoming lost in his own memories. Others who had experienced similar events became involved in their own thoughts as well. Matt spoke loudly to bring himself and others back to the present.

"I tried to provide comfort to myself and that young man by reading a psalm of David. Psalm 27 to be exact."

He lowered his eyes for a brief moment before lifting them again toward the church full of people. "But, I didn't finish it. The young man died, and I walked away, leaving my trust in a God I considered to be absent behind me." A single tear rolled down Paul Gentry's cheek.

"I felt that God had abandoned me, that young soldier, and every soldier who died in that war or any other war, so I replaced my faith with anger and my hope with resentment. I removed my trust and put distance between myself and God. I closed my eyes to the workings of God in our world and in our lives."

Naomi held Joe's hand tightly. Matt had shared this story only one time upon his return from the war, and it was after she and Joe had helped him recover from a particularly bad bout of anxiety. The memory became fresh in her mind, making her excitement combine with worry for the well-being of her dear friend. Joe placed his free hand over hers and winked at her in reassurance. He knew there was nothing for them to be concerned over.

Matt stepped down and stood in front of the Baron. "In these last few days, my eyes have been opened, and I have seen the presence of God all around us." His face showed excitement and happiness. "A young girl came into our town earlier this week with nothing more to her name than a bad attitude. In getting to know her, I started to see myself for what I had become. She was not afraid to call me out on my shortcomings, and she tested me concerning my faith."

Dejectedly he added, "I failed her tests miserably." Albie rocked in her seat as she thought about Sarah, alone at the bus station. Matt continued, "Each time I was pressed, my thoughts returned to the loss and coldness of the war and, each time, I crumbled."

He found Joe and Naomi. "Today, after taking that young girl to the bus station without providing her with the words she needed, I realized my lack of faith had made me hollow and empty inside. I could no longer pass off the charade I had been performing." His eyes held a compassionate sorrow for not understanding this epiphany much earlier.

Matt went on, "This young lady needed me to provide her with the simple words that showed her I was able to forgive God, and possibly more importantly, that I was able to trust in God." He shook his head at his own stubbornness. "Yet, I denied her that comfort. In that denial, I let her leave all alone. I abandoned her."

A soft murmur began among the people in the sanctuary. Matt found Paul Gentry again and spoke as if speaking directly to him. "Yesterday, we lost Millie Gentry, a wonderful woman." He paused a moment out of respect for Millie's life and for Paul's loss.

"All of us knew Millie, and none of you would be surprised for me to tell you that in her death, Millie Gentry provided me with the key to my life." Paul smiled.

Matt continued, "She returned me to the Word of God that I had given up when I felt God had not spared her son."

He saw the children in the congregation. Some were paying attention. Others were coloring in books or asleep. He scanned the faces of the mothers and knew they understood love like no other. He walked to the pulpit and held up the weathered, tattered, and stained Bible. A collective breath was drawn by the congregation.

He stepped to the side of the pulpit and grasped the Bible in his hand. "When I returned from the bus station, I was compelled to open this Bible." He placed his free hand on the Bible he was holding. "The book opened to the last page I had read. As I began to read the words of Psalm 27, I found God had never turned His back on me. I took my eyes off God and, ultimately, turned my back on Him."

He held out his hand in the motion of inclusion. "We are all capable of doing just that. We are prone to focus on the world of men." He looked at the Baron as he continued, "The world of men is relentless in its desires of the money, power, and tangible belongings. In a world where we only see the work and achievements of humans, we fall short of seeing the love of God."

He was hitting his stride, and he moved back down the aisle. "We blind ourselves to the glory and wonders of our ever-present God." For the first time in many, many services, an "Amen" rang out from the congregation.

Matt was energized by the motivation of the Holy Spirit. "The way of life in the world where the focus is only on human achievement is easier. The choices are not as hard, and the results are immediate. Gratification is quick and measurable." He paused at the end of the aisle and turned, "But we want more. We are not satisfied."

He began making his way back. "I was reminded in reading the psalm to look in the world for the goodness of God." He pointed his finger in the air. "I was reminded to open my eyes to the bigger story that surrounds each of us." He tried to make eye contact with as many people as he could as he made his way up the aisle.

"Those in this world who are blinded, search for power in themselves or over others. They are without substance because they lack faith." The Baron's face became red, and anger burned from his eyes, but Matt looked directly at him, standing only feet from him.

"I know, because I was blind. It is easy to proclaim belief without true faith. It is easy to look to yourself when you do not trust others. But it leaves one empty and unfulfilled." The Baron showed no response, but maintained a cold stare fixed upon the preacher.

Matt moved side to side in front of the pews. "Having faith allows us to make the harder choice and enables us to persevere against the largest of odds. Having faith allows our eyes to open, and it allows us to see the world outside ourselves and to experience the wonderful grace of God present in it."

Raising his voice, he said, "Showing trust and acting on faith opens our hearts and souls to the many blessings of God!"

Many "Amens" rang from the congregation after this last statement. Matt even heard Albie's definitive, "Mmmmm-huh" in the mix. "I denied forgiveness to myself and I refused God's forgiveness through our Savior, Jesus Christ, by doing so."

Matt continued, "God forgave me a long time ago, and I never asked for it. Now I sit in that salvation, and I see God in each one of you and in myself. I am renewed in my spirit and in my faith."

His voice became louder and filled with excitement as he stated, "I have strength through God, and I have resilience in His Word! My complete trust is placed in God, and I will never doubt again. I say to you all, 'Wait on the Lord: be of good courage, and he shall strengthen thine heart: wait, I say, on the Lord!'" "Amens" rang from the congregation, and hands were raised to the heavens with shouts of praise.

Matt looked out over the faces of those he cared so deeply for. "You are slaves to no man. You are children of God and are bathed in the love of His grace. Accept this grace with your faith in God and in the expression of your love of God and of others."

He bowed his head. "Let's go to God in prayer." All the heads, except one, lowered in the congregation. The Baron's cold stare had not shifted.

"Holy God, we are rich in our lives of Your heavenly abundance. Help us to keep our eyes on You and our hearts filled with Your glory. And all God's people said ..." Together, all of the people in congregational unison exclaimed, "Amen!"

Mrs. Carlton must have felt the Holy Spirit moving in the room. Her fingers moved across the keys of the old upright piano and began to play, "How Great Thou Art" in a joyous tone. Immediately the congregation stood and began to join in song. Each voice added to the beautiful melody of the hymn as, for the first time in a long time, praise rang loudly from the little church.

Matt was greeted by handshakes and smiles as he began to make his way down the aisle. He approached Joe and Naomi, but was stopped in his progress by Jesse Barrister. Standing in front of Matt was the Baron, whose scowling face revealed gritted teeth beneath his thick, gray mustache.

He puffed out his chest and wagged a pointed finger in the preacher's face. "You will never preach in my church again!"

Matt laughed and replied, "I don't need to. This church doesn't belong to you. It belongs to God and all His people." The Baron's eyes blazed with fury, and he began to challenge Matt once more, but Matt moved to the side of him and stepped forward.

As he passed, he put his hand on the Baron's shoulder and told him, "It is just a matter of perspective, Jesse." Matt moved on, and Jesse Barrister stood in disbelief.

Naomi greeted Matt with a hug, and Joe smacked his good friend on the back so hard it almost knocked the wind out of him. Duke, excited by the electricity moving through the church, came running from his seat upon seeing Matt.

Albie found her way to the group. "Now, that is the man we've been missing," she said as she wrapped her arms around Matt in a bear hug.

Matt laughed, then he held Albie by her shoulders. "Do you mind watching Duke for a bit?"

"You know I don't mind that old dog," said Albie. "I feed him better than you anyway." Then her face became more serious and she asked, "Why?"

Matt looked at Joe and Naomi, then answered, "I think I have a bus to catch."

Chapter 31

It had been more than an hour since Sarah had heard the second ringing of the church bells. The sun had set, and the moon had taken its place on the opposite horizon. She looked up to the sky and saw only the brightest of stars through the shining streetlights of the town square.

When she was a young girl, her father had sung her the song, "When You Wish upon a Star," before bed. It was a memory filed far back in her mind, and it was not one she could fully recollect. She tried hard for a moment to bring the full vision to her thoughts, but became frustrated by the inability to do so. There was a gentle breeze that blew the nighttime air, and she suspected that a midnight shower was on the way. She only hoped the bus arrived before the rain.

A car she did not recognize pulled up in front of her. The lights on the car blinded her so she could only see the silhouette of the driver. Putting her hand up to shield her eyes from the lights, she stood, hoping the higher angle would give her a better view.

The driver turned the lights off and shut off the engine. The door opened and a man in a fedora stepped from the car. Sarah was unsure what to do—part of her wanted to run, but the other part of her was curious as to who this person was and what he or she wanted. Her night vision began to return, and the mysterious driver stepped into the yellow light of the streetlamp on the curb.

"How ya doing?" the mayor asked with a wave. Relieved, Sarah let go of the breath she was holding, but then offered a quizzical look in reply. Just then a familiar pickup truck pulled into the space beside the mayor.

Matt emerged from the truck with a grand smile on his face. He looked at the funny little mustached man, "Mayor," he said with a nod.

"Preacher," the mayor responded. Matt moved from his truck and closed the distance between himself and Sarah. She said nothing as he moved closer. She was happy he was there, but she also knew he was going to try to deter her from leaving, and in that he would not succeed.

Matt stopped in front of her. "Sarah," he said softly, "I am sorry for being weak when you needed me to be strong." Sarah positioned her head to one side and studied him in the incandescent light. There was something different, something that had not been present when she first studied him at the diner. She felt coldness in his eyes then, but now they only showed compassion.

"Uh, okay," she responded, somewhat uncomfortable by his unfamiliar approach.

Matt motioned toward the bench where Sarah had been sitting. They both moved to the bench and took a seat. The mayor kept his distance and leaned on the front fender of his car, looking away from Matt and Sarah.

"The most wonderful thing happened at the service this evening," Matt began excitedly. "The Holy Spirit took hold of people, and folks were joyful and connected to God in worship." Sarah just stared at Matt.

"You don't understand, Sarah," Matt said, seeing her disinterest. "We have not worshipped like that in years." He looked out over the square and caught the mayor listening to them and smiling at Matt's story. The mayor quickly turned away. Sarah still said nothing and looked down at her hands in her lap.

"Listen," Matt said, deciding to take a different approach. "You asked me if I could forgive God." Sarah turned quickly and met his eyes. He continued, "It is a loaded question, Sarah. If I need to forgive God, that means I must blame God. So, your first question to me should be, 'Do you blame God?'"

Sarah, showing more interest, asked, "Do you?"

Matt nodded, "I did. I thought all of the horrible things I had seen and all of the death I had experienced was God's fault."

"Wasn't it?" asked Sarah.

"The answer to that question has plagued me for many years," Matt replied.

A rush of air moved past them, and the glimmer of the silver-sided bus could be seen approaching them on the street. The mayor looked at his watch and then raised his hands at Matt. The motion meant to ask Matt what he wanted to do. Matt's and Sarah's eyes followed the bus as it came to a stop in front of the building, behind Matt's truck and the mayor's car.

In a more urgent voice Matt continued, "We have the option in our lives to keep moving toward God and making choices that bring us closer to God." Matt could tell Sarah was distracted by the bus door opening and the exchange between the mayor and the driver.

He touched her arm, and she turned his way, "When we make the choices that bring us closer to God, we can accept the redemption, the salvation, and the forgiveness we have in Jesus. Then we find the strength to forgive ourselves and others. In forgiving ourselves, we find forgiveness from God because we are accepting all of the grace He has given us. I made a choice that took me away from God. I chose to not trust God anymore."

Sarah shook her head. "It is too much for me … I don't understand." She stood and looked over at the bus, "I have to go,

Matt." Matt was rushed and needed more time; he sighed and rose to his feet.

He yelled over the motor of the running bus, "Mayor!" The mayor turned his head, and Matt waved, then motioned for him to come over. The mayor said something to the driver, and the driver nodded, then the mayor walked quickly over to Matt and Sarah.

"Mayor, I am going to need that ticket," Matt said. The mayor nodded and went straight to the door and pulled out his key. Sarah watched, stunned, as Matt walked by her and followed the mayor into the entrance.

Matt was at the counter with the mayor on the opposite side when the door opened, ringing the bell inside the town hall. Both men turned and saw Sarah standing in the door way.

"As long as the door is open, may I use the restroom?" she asked. Matt looked at the mayor, and the mayor motioned her toward the ladies room with a thin smile. He pulled out the stamp and began working through the booklet when the door opened and the bell rang again. Matt turned back slowly, assuming that Sarah had gone back outside, but he was surprised to see his two friends standing in the doorway with travel bags in hand.

"Better add two more passengers, Mayor," Joe said with a grin. Naomi smiled.

Matt quickly went to his friends. "You don't have to go with me," he said.

"I know that, Matt," Joe replied. "I have been working on that farm for years without a break, Preacher." He puffed his chest. "I have earned a vacation."

Naomi laughed. Matt questioned her, "And you?"

She glanced at Joe and responded with a smirk, "You can learn a lot from other cultures, so I am choosing to expand my educational horizons."

Matt stepped back from them. "Vacation? Education? Fiddlesticks."

Sarah opened the side door and emerged into the main room of the town hall. She stopped in her tracks when she saw Naomi and Joe with their bags. Naomi saw her and took a couple of steps toward her.

"We couldn't let you leave alone," she said. Sarah moved to her in a near run and wrapped her arms around her. Naomi returned the embrace, wrapping her arms tightly around Sarah.

"Okay, gang," the mayor interrupted, "we need to get a move on. The driver would like to stay ahead of schedule." He handed Matt his ticket, and Matt and Sarah made their way outside.

As they opened the door, they were greeted by a light sprinkling of rain and the increased humidity of a brewing Texas thunderstorm. Matt ran to his truck and pulled a bag from the bed. Sarah flung her duffel bag over her back. Hurriedly the two made their way onto the bus and watched from the windows as Joe and Naomi got caught in a harder shower as they ran from the building to the bus door.

The bus was empty except for the four new passengers and the driver. The driver knew he had all of his passengers aboard and, as a result, he could leave earlier than the planned midnight departure.

Joe and Naomi sat in the seat in front of Matt and Sarah. It seemed odd to the driver having the four of them sit so close together in a bus that was so big and so empty. But they did not even notice the expanse of space around them. They were content being close and felt comforted by the presence of each other.

The bus driver closed the door, and Matt watched out the window as they pulled away from the town hall. Through the rain, he watched the mayor wave from beside his car. Matt raised his hand in a half wave, knowing the mayor was not able to see him through the soaked glass.

The four sat in silence as the bus traveled on the back roads toward the interstate. The rain, coming down much heavier, beat on the metal roof and against the windows, creating a hypnotic rhythm. The sound made them all drowsy and their eyes began to close.

Suddenly, remembering his mission, Matt opened his eyes and turned to Sarah. She was nearly asleep when he woke her. "It was not God's fault, Sarah."

"What?" she asked, annoyed at him waking her. He no longer cared what she thought of him; the focus was on her finding the God that longed for His lost child in her.

He spoke directly and passionately. "In one moment, it can seem like our lives are perfect. It is easy to see the work of a loving God around us. But life can get difficult, and things become more complicated. Our world can become darker, making it harder to see God's work and making it seem more difficult to experience God's love.

"Those are the times, Sarah. Those are the times when we have to show our greatest trust in God. We have to believe, despite the worst situation, that God's love will persevere. Our faith in knowing that God is present and at work can give us strength and courage to get through the turmoil surrounding us."

He turned his shoulders so he faced the young girl and tried to simplify his thoughts. "Love, Sarah. That is all. That is the only thing that God asks of us. He asks us to love Him, and He asks us to love one another."

Joe and Naomi both turned in their seats. "I can't argue with that," Joe said.

"I would have to agree," Naomi added.

"Why do you suppose that is?" asked Matt. Sarah shrugged.

"Love is a powerful thing," said Naomi. She smiled at Joe, and he returned the gesture.

"Love is the foundation of our faith and root of our hope," Matt offered. Joe and Naomi nodded in agreement. "If we are able to love God only a tiny bit as unconditionally as God loves us, then our faith in God will grow stronger," Matt said passionately.

"Spoken like a true preacher," Joe said out of the corner of his mouth. Matt rolled his eyes, and Naomi gave an admonishing look.

"Sarah," Matt said in a strong and fatherly tone, "I am only going to say this once, and I want you to think about it for what it means to you. Love of God means choosing God and God's ways in our life. God has already chosen us. Even when things go wrong, and it seems that we are being separated from God, God is pulling us closer to Him and asking us to trust in His grace. He is using the power of His love to show us the way home to Him."

He was sounding like a preacher again, but the fact that his words were not empty was not lost on Sarah. He paused until she looked at him. "Until you arrived in town this week, I had made every decision to turn from God and to keep myself distant from Him and blame Him for my misery. It was easier to live life relying on myself than to face the fact that it was I who had lost my trust and pushed God away."

With emphasis, Matt added, "Sometimes—most times—the easiest path is not the right one. So, we need God to give us the courage and strength to take the harder journey. And Sarah, God will always be with us. Even if we leave Him, God never leaves us. For every wrong, we are forgiven. God became human in Jesus Christ and suffered and died so we could experience eternal love and life."

He looked adoringly at the young girl and joyfully encouraged her, "Choose love, Sarah. Choose grace. Have trust. And you will experience the power of God in awesome and wonderful ways."

Suddenly, lights flooded the cabin of the bus and a sounding horn vibrated the air. The passengers had no time to react in any way. Not even a scream could be heard as the side of the bus gave way to the front end of a semitruck. The sickening sound of metal bending and glass breaking replaced the tranquil stillness that had existed only moments before. The rain continued to drive down hard upon the bus, but without the barriers intact, the weather found its way inside, making all it touched cold and wet.

The impact slammed the two men into the ladies beside them and spread shattered glass and twisted metal through the air. The front wheels of the semi turned as the engine whirled loudly in the broken compartment of the bus. The bus's frame gave way to the force of the impact and crumpled, causing it to fall on its side. Its wheels turned freely underneath the load the tractor trailer was carrying.

The cab of the truck rested high in the air on the side of the bus, as if on some strange lift. The weight of the large engine pulled the cab of the truck down through the floor of the bus until it rested only feet from the passengers. The bus filled with smoke and fumes from the diesel fuel spilling onto the ground.

Joe had been flipped completely upside down by the accident, and he rested at a ninety-degree angle to Naomi. He could not feel any pain, and his sight was obscured by a warm liquid covering his face. He reached his hand above his head and moved it back and forth slowly until he felt the side of Naomi's face. He placed his hand gently on her cheek and silently waited for her to return his touch. There was no response.

His last thought was of the picture on Naomi's mantle of Joseph's graduation. Together they had raised a son, and together they had learned to love again. When he took his last breath, he was happy.

Sarah came to and felt an enormous pain in her leg. She heard a groan and felt Matt beside her. She rolled to face him, grimacing from her discomfort. He was bleeding from his ears and from his mouth, but he looked at Sarah, and she saw nothing but love in his eyes.

His right arm was pinned under a displaced seat, but he moved his left arm as if searching for something. Grasping the side of his jacket, he pulled the flap up on his pocket and retrieved something from inside.

Matt was barely able to speak when he placed the leather, bloodstained Bible in Sarah's hand. Sarah began to cry, and she put her face against Matt's. "Sarah," he said faintly but with excitement, "it is beautiful. It is wonderful. God is with us ..." Then his eyes grew wide, and life left his body.

Sarah wailed loudly from the loss and the pain. She felt herself grow weak and tired, and all went black.

~~~

The police report indicated that the sudden heavy rain had caused a stop sign to be washed out from the intersection. The bus and the 18-wheeler entered the crossroads without slowing. Both drivers had miraculously survived the impact.

The bus driver had been far enough ahead of the point of impact to escape with only bumps and bruises. Although the truck driver's physical ailments were more serious, he too walked away from the scene. The four passengers on the bus were not that fortunate.

In memorial to the loss of the lives of their beloved friends, the folks in town erected three permanent wooden crosses on the side of the intersection. Since the names of the three friends were on their grave markers, the town voted to honor them in a more collective fashion. The crosses each stated one different word: "Teacher," "Farmer," and "Preacher."

Epilogue

2012

The church was silent as Pastor Jones finished telling his story. He could hear the sniffles and see the tears of his visibly shaken congregation. Obviously they had not expected such a tragic ending to the story he had been sharing. He stayed silent for only seconds longer before continuing.

"Sarah was badly injured in the accident, but she did not die," he said with happiness. "She woke in an Austin hospital," he continued. Then he paused to ask a question. "Who do you think was in the room with her when she woke?"

More than half of his listeners responded correctly. "Albie," they said gleefully.

"That's right. Sarah woke, and Albie was knitting by the side of her bed," he told them. "Not only her, but she had put a service dog vest on Duke, and he slept on the floor beside her."

"Sarah felt comfort at seeing them, but as her mind cleared, the first thing she thought of was the Bible Matt had given her. She looked around the room frantically for the leather book. She did not see it, and tears came to her eyes."

Pastor Jones continued his story, "Albie saw her distress and reached into a bag beside her on the floor. She handed Sarah the old, leather, bloodstained Bible. And like the others before her, Sarah took the Bible and held it close to her chest."

Pastor Jones had been able to make his way through his sermon without getting choked up, but now he struggled to keep his emotions at bay.

"As they prepared to leave the hospital, Albie asked Sarah if they needed to get a ticket to Mexico. Sarah looked at Albie and said, 'No, I would like to go home. Our home.' Albie gave Sarah a great, big smile and said, 'Mmmm-huh.'" The congregation laughed.

"Upon exiting the hospital, they were greeted by Joseph, who held a familiar pipe between his teeth. He loaded them in his father's old Buick and drove them to the small West Texas town. Albie treated Sarah as if she was her own child, and their relationship grew to be strong and rooted in the love of God of which Preacher Matt had spoken," Pastor Jones was proud to share.

"The town came to adopt Sarah as well. They often talked about how her arrival had brought with it a rejuvenation of the Spirit. In the tragedy of death, the town came together in new life."

With joy he shared, "Nearly seven months later, the two women—and Duke—greeted Sarah's little boy. She named him Matthew Joseph Jones." It only took a moment for the name recognition to set in. There were audible gasps as people now understood the implication of the date.

Pastor Jones reached into his pulpit and pulled from it a tattered and torn leather Bible. He opened the Bible to Psalm 27 and held it above his head. The bloodstain still remained visible on the pages, and reactions varied in the room. Some shouted, "Amen," while others bowed their heads in prayer, and still others simply stared in disbelief.

"Preacher Matt gave this book to my mother the day he died, and he, Joe, and Naomi saved her life and mine. She read this book to me every night, and because Matt, Naomi, Joe, and Albie showed my mother God's love, she was able to show it to me."

Pastor Jones held out his hands, and the congregation became still. Pulling the Bible in front of him, he read from Psalm 27:14, "Wait on the Lord: be of good courage, and he shall strengthen thine heart: wait, I say, on the Lord."

He lowered the Bible and looked into the congregation until he found a particular woman sitting in the front row. Her hair was gray, and she wore a beautiful wide-brimmed hat and a floral dress that she had always been fond of. Crossing her legs, she revealed a new pair of angel-wing embroidered boots. He smiled at her and mouthed the words, "Thank you." Sarah smiled back and pointed to the sky.